A LOOK AT LOVE

He pulled Aggie over and began kicking straw from the stack, spreading it around on the ground. He did not let go of her, his big hands hopping here, there, clutching, pinching, rubbing.

Aggie became interested. They kissed. Aggie was hugging him now, moaning low in her throat.

Jodie glanced at Easter. Easter was staring at the lovers, her eyes wide, her mouth slightly open.

Suddenly, Buzz picked Aggie up, held her in his arms, kissed her on the belly. Aggie moaned and Buzz dropped down to the bed of straw he had made with his feet.

Jodie glanced at Easter again, and found her staring at him. As their eyes met, she wriggled around, on to her side, and put her arms around him.

"Oh," she sighed, "how can I stand it? Oh, I— I feel like I'm going to smother. Oh, Jodie hon! Oh, Jodie, sweet!" She pushed her face beneath his chin and kissed him on the neck. "Please, Jodie!" She was hugging him, tugging at him . . .

the
BARN

glenn low

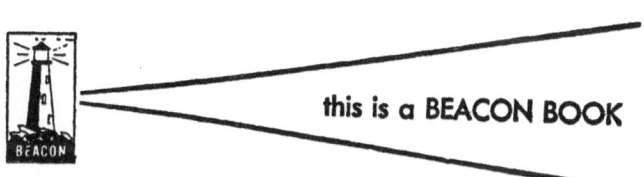

this is a BEACON BOOK

WILDSIDE PRESS

1

HE was certain about it now. It was the stillness, and the way the starlight looked so brittle, as if it would shatter into millions of tiny pieces if he pushed his fist into it too hard, that gave him the feeling . . . He stopped walking and stood in the middle of the dusty road, and thought about the feeling. It was like a voice speaking his name over and over again, warning him of some terrible danger. It did not make good sense. Trying to disregard it, he lifted his head and looked at the barn.

He figured that this was the Danson place, all right. Ruie had said it was the first farm on the river road west of the covered bridge.

"A big two-story house, painted white and trimmed in green," she had said. "It stands a good ways back from the road. The barn stands on the road, though. And the lane goes in right beside it. The mailbox is on a tall post across the lane from the barn. You can't miss it, Jodie. My papa's name is on the mailbox in big black letters. Jason Danson."

Jodie Saylem walked over to the corner of the barn and put down the suitcase, got a book of matches from his jacket pocket. He ripped out a match, then looked down the lane at the house. Four front windows, two upstairs and two down, showed light through yellow blinds. Funny, he thought, that they would pull the blinds all the way down in the downstairs front room. . . .

5

He glanced across the lane at the mailbox—it was there, on a tall post, exactly as Ruie had said it would be. "Must be the right place," he murmured, and went across to the mailbox. He did not need the match. The starlight let him see the name on the mailbox plainly enough. JASON DANSON. He dropped the match, went back and picked up the suitcase. He saw the dog then, and stiffened. It was a large dog, and vicious-looking, even in death.

Jodie squatted beside it and pushed back the lane-side weeds, and was astonished. "Throat's cut," he muttered, and laid a hand on the animal's belly. "Still warm . . . Must have been killed only a few minutes ago."

He rose and stood tall, and peered at the house. "My God," he whispered. "A person that'd kill a dog that way—a person that'd do a cruel thing like that—"

He took three hesitant steps down the lane, then halted abruptly as he heard someone giggle. The giggle lasted for only a second or two, then there was silence, except for the breath scratching in Jodie's throat. He gulped at the scratching sound, and a cold, mushy feeling lumped in his stomach. He stood stone-still and listened.

The giggle had stopped almost as soon as it started, but the sound of it went on in his memory. He guessed a girl had made it. "Whoever she is," he told himself, trying to give more depth to his listening, "she's not alone. She couldn't be and giggle like that. If—if it's Ruie and—and some guy . . . If it is, goddamn her! . . . If it is, what'll I do? What can I do?"

He put the suitcase down as quietly as he could, and stood hunched over it, hands knotted into fists, teeth gritting together, and thought of his car back by the covered bridge, parked in the weeds beside the road with a dead ignition coil. If the damned old wreck had not stalled, he would have got here before dark and likely would not have heard the giggle—would not feel

6

miserable, sick, and like he was going crazy, the way he felt now.

"But maybe it's for the best," he suddenly decided. "Because if Ruie's in the barn there monkey-doodling with some guy, I guess I ought to know about it. I guess—"

The giggle came again, and Jodie winced as though someone had slapped him across the mouth. This time what he heard was different, with the giggle running into laughter, and the laughter continuing long enough for him to get its full significance—the hot, lewd flavor of it.

"My God!" he said huskily, and licked his lips. "My God! If that is Ruie and some fellow in there, I'll—I'll—"

Sudden excruciating awareness of his age and inexperience swept over him, and for an awful moment he had the degrading feeling that he was going to blubber. He clenched his teeth, shook his head, and the feeling passed.

He stood in the barn's shadow, and could not see if there was a door in its nearest wall. "I got to find out if it's Ruie," he told himself. "I got to find out, goddamn it!"

He sighed and swore again, this time silently, and leaned heavily against the dark wall. What did he want, anyway? Did he want to go in there and catch Ruie, the girl he was going to marry, in some strange fellow's arms—face her down, tell her off? Was that what he wanted? There could be serious trouble if he went in there and did that. The guy might jump him, or he might lose his head and jump the guy. He or the guy might get hurt, both of them might get hurt, one of them might get killed, even . . . He had one hell of a temper; he had to remember that.

What if he were only nineteen? He was bigger and stronger than most men. He was plenty big and strong enough to beat a guy to death, if he got the upper hand and lost his temper. Jodie gave his head a hard shake and swished his tongue back and forth across his lips, and gulped. How dry his mouth and throat were! It hurt him just to swallow. "I got to find out," he told himself. "By God, I got to know if it's Ruie in there. That's all there is to it. I got to find out!"

He straightened up and felt of the wall, felt of it from the nearest corner to as far as he could reach, then crept and felt of it all the way along to the rear of the barn. No door, no window, on this side. He paused, listened for a moment, heard nothing except the murmur of insects, the distant cry of an owl. Then he moved around the corner, out into the star-glow. Here he paused again, listened, looked all around.

Now he was by the wall that faced toward the house. The stock door and a high-set window were on this side. The barn lot joined here. There were two late-model sedans parked in the barn lot. Jodie remained motionless for a long moment, staring at the cars—wondering if the laughter could have come from one of them. They appeared to be empty, but he could not see inside them clearly enough to tell for sure.

Then, abruptly, the giggle came again, and he knew a girl had made it, and that she was not in either of the sedans. She was in the barn, not far from the stock door that was standing slightly ajar.

"It's Ruie," he told himself angrily, despairingly. "It's Ruie, all right. The dirty little cheat!"

He got the book of matches from his jacket, carefully tore off a match, pressed its head against the striking surface, then moved on, keeping close to the wall. He was going to step inside the barn, strike the match, see who was here and what was going on. . . . But he did not do it. Just before he reached the door, he heard a man's voice, and stopped, listened, as it said:

"I'll tear them. I will. I mean it. You uncross your

8

legs or I'll tear them. They feel like very expensive panties, too."

The girl gave a teasing, throaty laugh. She did not speak so Jodie could try to tell if she were Ruie Danson or not. She only laughed, and the way she laughed told him the fellow wouldn't have to tear her panties to get them off her. The laughter stopped. There were a few seconds of dead silence. Then the girl gave a soft, long-drawn moan.

Jodie gritted his teeth and cursed in his soul, listening to it, and thought, Ruie moans like that sometimes. When she wants it real bad, she does. Oh, damn her, the damn bitch.

The moan ended on a sigh, then came again. Then there was a mumbled "Ummm . . . Ummm . . ." Then the sound of hard, pulling kisses.

"Maybe I'll kill her," Jodie told himself. "Maybe I'll kill them both."

Urgent rustling sounds were coming from the barn now, and he guessed the couple were romping, embracing, on straw or hay. Soon there were sharply drawn breaths. The romping, struggling noises continued. All at once—he did not know exactly when it began—he was aware of the girl saying, murmuring over and over, "Oh, Gary! . . . Gary . . . Gary . . . Gary . . . Oh! . . ." Oh, Gary, darling! Darling . . . darling . . . darling . . . Oh! . . .

He said to himself, desperately, "If she only would speak a little louder. If she only would speak out in a normal tone of voice. If she only would, so I could be certain. So I'd know—so I'd know what to do."

He could go in there and strike a match as he had planned. He could find out if she were Ruie that way. And that was what he would do in a very few seconds, if—

Something moved.

Over there between the sedans, something moved—

9

something slim and upright and pale—something that looked like a naked human figure ...

A fleeting glimpse was all he had had. Then it had vanished. But it was still there, between the sedans. It had to be. It had moved in there, and it had not come out.

Jodie remembered the dog with its throat cut, lying in the bloody weeds. He licked his lips, found them cold and stiff, and went on staring at the sedans—thinking how strange they should be here—new, expensive cars like those, parked in a poor dirt farmer's barn lot. ... He remembered the blinds at the two front downstairs windows—they had been pulled all the way down.

He stiffened as the girl in the barn let out a sudden, thick, grunting scream.

The scream set him to trembling all over. He licked his lips, tried to swallow, and could not. God, how dry his mouth and throat were! God, how his knees were shaking! What was wrong with him? Was he afraid? Was he just now finding out that he was a coward?

He guessed he was only unnerved. He did not know. But one thing he did know—that monkey-doodling in the barn was over with, at last. The girl's throaty scream had told him it was. For he had heard Ruie cry out like that. He had made her cry out like that. ...

"By God, if it's Ruie, I ought to kill her!" he breathed. "If it's Ruie I ought to kill her and the fellow, too. And maybe I will."

But what had he seen over there between the sedans? A human being? If it were a human being, was it hiding there now, watching him? He drew a deep breath slowly. "To hell with it," he told himself. "I'm going in there and—"

They were coming out. He heard their feet moving through straw or hay, heard their voices, low, incomprehensible. But they were coming out. Now he would learn what he had to know.

Quickly, stealthily, he moved back around the corner

10

of the barn, back to where he had been, in the shadow. He felt certain the girl was Ruie, and he cautioned himself against acting hastily, making a fool of himself. There would be plenty of time to do whatever he decided to do after they came out—after he knew for sure the girl was Ruie, and knew what the fellow was like. "He's likely bigger and older than I am," he told himself. "Likely I won't stand a chance of whipping him. But I'll try to whip him if I think I ought. Try my damndest."

It struck him that he was thinking like a punk kid, and he was ashamed. What was wrong with him, anyway? He was almost twenty. He was six feet tall and weighed around one-ninety. He certainly was not any weakling. He had earned a scholarship in football at Greening U., was going to enroll there this fall. So why was he afraid he could not handle this fellow? A lot of people, including sportswriters for the newspapers, considered him the best, toughest fullback Stallerville High had ever had.

Besides, this fellow might be a little, scrawny, cowardly punk. . . . It might turn out that he would be ashamed to even so much as punch him in the nose.

Jodie was watching the barn door so intently that he almost missed seeing what happened over by the sedans. He glimpsed it, though—a pale, moving blur, like someone, or something, running from behind the farthest sedan and disappearing around the corner of the barn. It could have been a calf or a sheep. . . . With such a brief look, he could not be certain. But he thought it was somebody, a half-grown boy, maybe, wearing light-colored clothes.

A moment later, he forgot about the blurry movement, as the barn door squeaked and the fellow stepped around it, out into the starlight.

He was a big guy, all right, and husky. He pulled the door all the way open, reaching behind him, and there

11

he was, as plain as anything, looking all around. He had a solid, settled look to him that let Jodie guess he must be at least thirty. He was not so tall, but Jesus, was he ever broad, especially across the shoulders! He was dressed like a businessman, in a hat and a dark suit. Jodie, looking him over, sighed and held his breath, and wondered why the girl did not come out.

He was still holding his breath when something sharp touched his back between his shoulders, and a voice, whispering, said, "Don't move. Don't make a sound. This is a knife you're feeling, buddy boy. Do as I say or I'll stick you with it, stick you deep."

As the words were spoken, the knife's point moved deeper and deeper into him. He considered making a quick, big, straight-ahead jump. But he stopped considering it when he remembered the dog with its throat cut in the weeds. He stood still.

A couple of seconds went by, then the voice whispered again, "That's oke, buddy boy. Play it cool. That's very oke. Now you just back up a little. Easy . . . Step slowly, buddy boy."

The girl had not showed in the door. Lordy, but he wished she would! Lordy, but he needed to see her, needed to know if she were Ruie! Lordy, how he hated to do what the voice said! Never in his life had he hated doing a thing so much. But the knife was in his back for maybe a quarter of an inch. "Goddamn it!" he said through gritted teeth. He shook his head. "Goddamn you, too, whoever you are!" he whispered hoarsely. "You and your knife—goddamn you to hell!"

"Easy, buddy boy. Easy."

The girl was coming out—he heard her laugh. The fellow spoke to her. She said something, but Jodie could not make it out. Then Jodie saw her, but not clearly enough to tell if he knew her. She slipped her arm beneath the fellow's, and they went out of the doorway, walking close together. They went across the corner of the barn lot, passed behind the sedans, and entered the lane, heading toward the house.

Jodie could see only their backs. The girl wore dark clothes. She was Ruie's size and build; but, damn it, he could not tell if she were Ruie or not. And now, damn his miserable luck, he probably never would know who she was.

The voice whispered again, and it and the knife took him backwards along the wall and around the front corner of the barn. Then, with the barn between them and the house, the voice said, "We stop here. You can turn around now."

They stopped. The knife left his back. "But please don't yell or throw any punches or do anything crazy," the voice said. "Just thank me for getting you away from out there in time. Gary might have spotted you."

Jodie turned around, and stiffened with surprised. He wanted to laugh and he wanted to cuss. But mostly he wanted to look. The whispering had fooled him completely. He had been under the impression that he was dealing with a man, and here it was only a girl, and a half-pint girl at that. He stared at her, too shocked to speak until he realized his mouth was hanging open —then he closed it, cleared his throat, and said, "Who are you, anyway? Do you go around like that all the time, or did somebody swipe your clothes?"

She smiled up at him. She was the palest blonde he had ever seen. Her hair—she wore it in a long bob— was as pale as the skimpy, thigh-length garment she was wearing. And the garment was pearly white. She had large, soft eyes—he guessed they were blue—and a small face that curved delicately to a tiny chin. Her mouth was small, too, but ripe, full-lipped, and sweetly shaped.

Her smile stopped. A dimple showed. She said, "I was going to ask you the same thing. But now I won't.

13

Because I'm sure I know who you are. You're Ruie's one and only—Jodie Saylem."

"Who are you?" he repeated.

"I'm Easter," she replied. "Don't tell me Ruie never told you about me."

He stared at her. He did not believe it. "Easter—you?"

She nodded. The dimple appeared and the smile came back. He moved closer to her, still staring at her. "Ruie's sister—you?" he said.

"Yes."

She went on smiling, but now the smile was not right, somehow. He got the impression that she was suddenly remembering that she was frightened.

He tried to bring to mind all that Ruie had told him about her. It was not much; he thought he remembered it all. He caught himself staring at the knife in her hand. It was an old-fashioned carving knife with a long, curved blade. He could not see to tell, but he guessed it had a curved handle, too. He thought of the dead dog, and almost shuddered.

"Something's wrong around here," he said. "Why—why are you—" He was staring at the skimpy, thigh-length garment as he paused.

She moved back three steps, watching him, then glanced around the corner of the barn, looking toward the house. "Something is wrong," she said, and moved back, stood close in front of him. "Something very awful is wrong, Jodie. That's why I had to use the knife to make you come here with me, so I could tell you about it. You can't see Ruie now, Jodie. Not tonight, maybe not tomorrow or tomorrow night. They won't let her leave the house, and, of course, you don't dare go to her—not till Walt comes and they all leave."

He had been about to say he had just seen Ruie and that he did not want to see her again, ever. But that had been before he had heard Easter out. "Who won't let Ruie leave the house?" he asked, trying not to stare at Easter's pretty legs. "Why don't I dare to go to her? And who's Walt?"

She answered the last question first, frowning. "Walt's my brother—Ruie's brother. Didn't Ruie tell you she had a brother?"

"No," he replied, thinking how little he really knew about Ruie Danson. He had met her only three months ago when she had come to Stallerville to work as a bookkeeper for her uncle, who owned the Stallerville Feed and Fuel Company. He had fallen in love with her after their first date, and she had seemed to fall in love with him. On their third date, he had asked her to marry him and she had said she would, any time. He had set the day, after she had declined to do so—a day thirteen months ahead, the day after his twenty-first birthday.

He was thinking now that most of their time together had been spent in physical communication, very little of it in talking, in getting really acquainted. She certainly had not ever mentioned having a brother named Walt. She had told him that her mother was dead, had spoken of Easter several times, had mentioned her father once or twice. It surprised him to realize that he knew Ruie only in one way, and that in every other way she was a stranger to him.

"I'm not surprised she didn't tell you about Walt," Easter said. "Walt's the black sheep of the family. He's an ex-con. Did time in the big house for armed robbery. He was let out on parole about a year ago." She paused, watching his face intently. He did not speak.

She drew a deep breath and went on. "It's Walt's fault I'm out here like this, with nothing on but my pajama top. It's his fault old Syl's dead with his throat cut from ear to ear. It's his fault that Buzz and Gary and those two tramps—that Aggie and that Emma—

15

are in our house right now. This whole awful mess is his fault."

She gave him a quick smile, but he knew now that the smile was only an attempt to hide the fear that was almost driving her into hysterics.

"You heard Gary and Emma in the barn awhile ago," she said. "Buzz and Aggie were in the barn doing the —the same thing, and only about an hour after they all got here, too."

He stared at her, wondering if she were lying to protect Ruie. He looked at the knife in her hand. "Where'd you get that?" he asked.

"From the meat house out back of the house," she told him.

He hoped she was not lying about some girl named Emma being in the barn just now with the husky guy. "Who owns those cars parked in the barn lot?" he asked.

"I don't know for sure. Gary and Buzz, I guess. Buzz and Aggie came here in one, Gary and Emma in the other."

"And your brother Walt, is he here?"

She shook her head. "No. He hasn't been here for three weeks. But he's due here tonight." She paused, moved a step closer, so close he could have reached out and taken her in his arms.

"Oh, Jodie," she said, and he thought she was going to start crying. "I—I have to tell you all about it, and—and I don't want to. It's just too horrible."

"They're crooks, huh—that Buzz and Gary?"

She nodded. "Yes. The very worst kind of crooks. They kidnapped a little girl and brought her here. Oh, Jodie, it's—it's too awful to even think about."

"Kidnapped a—is she—is she here now, in your house?"

"Yes. They brought her here tonight in Buzz's car— tied up and gagged and packed in the luggage compartment. And she's—she's frightened almost crazy. And she's such a sweet, delicate little thing. Only sixteen. I saw her when they carried her upstairs and put her on the bed in Walt's room. I was in my room—it's just across the hall from Walt's—peeping through a crack in the door. After I saw them and the girl, heard what they said, and knew what they were up to, I got out of there, climbed out the window onto the back porch roof and—and—"

"How long ago was that?" Jodie interrupted.

"Right after dark, about an hour ago, I guess. I went out back and hid on top of the straw stack there, behind the cow stable, and watched the house for a long time. Then when Buzz and Aggie came out and came down here to the barn, I got off the straw stack and sneaked over here to see what they were up to. And —and I found out pretty quick. Golly, did I!"

"How many in the house besides them and the kidnapped girl?" Jodie asked, wondering why she had not gone to the nearest farm and sent someone to fetch the sheriff. He knew there was no telephone service this far back in the hills. Ruie had said so last week when she had told him she was coming here for a short visit, and he had said he would give her a ring in a couple of days.

"Papa's place is miles from a telephone, Jodie," she had said. "So we won't be in touch till next Friday when you drive out to fetch me home. And don't forget to pick up my suitcase at Uncle Rob's house. There are some presents in it I bought for Papa and Easter, also some things I'll need—clothes and stuff."

He had picked up the suitcase, at her Uncle Rob's. It was here, around the corner of the dark barn, in the weeds. . . .

"Papa and Ruie are the only ones in the house besides that poor, frightened girl," Easter was saying. "My mother's dead, long ago. Only Papa and I live here now, But I suppose Ruie told you—"

17

He told her about the suitcase, what was in it. "I'll get it," he said. "There's probably a skirt or something in it you can put on. A dress, maybe."

"Oh—I hope so."

"I'm going to the nearest farm and get someone to drive me to town," he said, moving past her, over to the corner of the barn. "I'll get word to the sheriff plenty quick about this. Don't worry. How close is the nearest phone?"

"About five miles," she said. "I didn't hear you drive in. You do have a car?"

He told her where his car was, what had happened to it.

She did not say anything. He waited for her to speak. Finally, she said, "The Fensers are our closest neighbors. Their place is five miles down the road. But you mustn't go there and tell them about this—this awful thing. Jodie, you mustn't. You mustn't tell anybody about it, yet."

"Why not?"

"Because of Papa. He'll be arrested along with the crooks if you do. He—he's mixed up in—in the kidnapping. He—he didn't want to be. But Walt made him be. Walt planned the whole mess. Walt's the leader. He meant to bring the Shetsher girl here right from the first. I heard Buzz tell Papa so, and I heard Papa say it was true. So if the others are arrested, so will Papa be. And, Jodie, he's not really guilty of anything. Walt forced him to let them bring the girl here. Walt was going to—Well, if you knew Walt, you'd know that Papa isn't to blame for what he did."

"Did you know about Walt's plans?" Jodie asked. "Did Ruie?"

"No. No, Ruie didn't know about them. I didn't either, not until I heard Papa and Buzz fussing tonight. Papa's not well, Jodie. He's got a bad heart. He'll die if he's put in jail. He'll probably die anyway, this awful thing happening here and him worrying so about it. Papa's a good man. Really he is, Jodie. It was Walt that—"

He interrupted her. "Do you know when they expect Walt to show up?"

"Tonight, they said. He stayed behind to collect the ransom. He'll skeedaddle out of Louisville just as soon as he gets it, I reckon."

"Louisville—is that where the girl lives?"

"Yes. I heard Buzz telling Papa all about it—when they expect Walt, and all."

"Do you think the girl will be turned loose when Walt gets here?"

She nodded, giving him a curious stare. "I guess so. I didn't hear any of them say. But the victim's always turned loose when the ransom is paid, isn't—"

He cut her short. "Not always. Sometimes the victim is killed. If it's the safest way."

"But they couldn't kill that sweet little girl," Easter said. "My God, Jodie, they couldn't do that!"

"They stole her, didn't they?" he said. "All right, they can kill her, then. They can kill her, all right."

2

THE straw stack behind the cow stable was the biggest, tallest one Jodie had ever seen. He climbed to the top of it, crouched in the hollow where Easter had been lying less than an hour ago, and looked all around. He was surprised to find that he could see the house, the barn, the other outbuildings, the parked sedans, and the road, all the way back to the covered bridge where he had left his car.

The starlight seemed brighter now than an hour ago,

19

and the warm night seemed to be turning warmer. He thought how nice it would be if he could lie down here in the clean straw and go to sleep. Then he wondered when he would be able to go to sleep again. "Not while Ruie's in there with those kidnappers," he told himself, staring at the house.

He had climbed up here after opening the suitcase for Easter and waiting until she found a blouse and skirt of Ruie's that suited her, and told him she would put them on if he would turn his back and not peep. "A bra and panties are in the suitcase," she had informed him, sounding embarrassed. "I guess I need them worse than anything."

He silently agreed. He had noticed, when he was behind her, sneaking over here from the barn, that she had nothing on except bedroom slippers and the pajama top. He had not tried to notice; he just had. She had stopped far over, and he had seen all there was to see of her from the waist down. He had felt ashamed to look; but, afterwards, thinking about it, he was not sorry he had. She was a beautifully built girl, more delightfully formed than Ruie, even. He had not seen her breasts, really, as the pajama top covered them; but once when she was stooping over and turned toward him, he had glimpsed enough of them to know how they were—very firm, large, but not too large, and pertly tilted. He had thrilled at the way they held the pajama top off her when she stood up straight, so that it did not touch her anywhere in front below them. Ruie had told him her age—eighteen, almost two years younger than Ruie. She was certainly a man's kind of a girl. . . .

Except for the kitchen, the rooms at the rear of the house were without light. He could not see the light in the kitchen, except where it showed on the full-drawn blinds at the two windows. Once he saw a man's shadow pass over the blinds, moving with head bent, and guessed it was the shadow of Jason Danson. He felt sorry for the aging farmer, remembering what Easter had said about him. He meant to get Danson out of the house along with Ruie, if he could.

"I oughn't to feel sorry for him, though," he told himself. "He didn't have to let them bring the girl here, no matter what his son said or did." He thought of his own father then, thought how difficult it would be for his father to turn him in to the law, no matter what the reason; and he considered how Ruie might feel toward him if he caused her father and brother to be sent to prison.

"I guess she'd come to despise me pretty quick," he told himself, and shook his head worriedly. He began trying to think of a way he could get Ruie, her father, and the kidnapped girl safely out of the house.

"If I could get them out of there and we could hide somewhere," he said, speaking the words slowly in his mind, "and if those crooks couldn't find us, I guess they'd leave after a while. And later we could all go in to the county seat, and I could tell the sheriff that the kidnappers, wanting a place to hide with the girl, had forced their way into the house; and I had got the girl and the Dansons away from them. That way Walt wouldn't need to be brought into it, and there would be no reason for the sheriff to suspect Mr. Danson. So— if I can only think of a way—"

In the cow stable a few yards away, a cow mooed softly, and over in the chickenhouse, a rooster flapped his wings and crowed. "Yeah—if I can only think of a way," Jodie mused. He turned from the hips, propped himself on his elbows and looked down across the straw stack's shaggy wall. He did not see Easter. He did not expect to; likely she was still dressing, and was keeping out of sight under the stack's overhang. She would be able to hear him though even if he spoke in a whisper.

He said in a low voice, "Easter—Easter, can you hear me?"

"Yes," came the half-whispered reply.

"Are you dressed?"

"No. I'm looking at the present Ruie bought for me. You should see it, Jodie. It's nice. A bath set. Soap and dusting powder and bubble bath crystals. Only— only just try to picture me using the stuff taking a bath in a big old tin washtub—"

He thought he heard her laugh. He could not be sure. He said, "Hurry and get dressed. I want to talk to you about the house—inside. How many rooms, how the rooms and the hall are laid out, where the stairs go up. Hurry, huh?"

"Okay."

He thought he heard a bumping noise over toward the house. He got up on his knees and looked that way. He was sure he had heard it, then. For the kitchen door was wide open and a man was standing in it, looking out—a big man with huge, sloping shoulders. "Must be Buzz," he told himself. Then: "He couldn't have heard us talking. It's too far. He's just getting a breath of fresh air, I figure."

Easter's voice said, louder than before, "I have a notion to unwrap Papa's present. It's not very big. I wonder what it is?"

Jodie twisted around and back, not taking his eyes off the man in the door. "Shhh!" he whispered. "Keep quiet."

Easter did not reply, so he guessed she had heard him. He settled back in the straw, watching the man, wondering.

A girl appeared behind the man. She looked out over his shoulder, then squeezed into the doorway beside him, put her arm around his waist. Jodie heard her speak, then laugh. He could not make out the words. The man laughed, a short, barking sound. Several seconds passed, then the man left the doorway, crossed the porch, stepped down in the yard and walked over to the gate in the picket fence. He stopped there and looked all around.

The girl spoke to him, and this time Jodie heard what she said. "Where you going, Buzz?"

The man answered her, but did not speak loudly enough for Jodie to understand him. He understood the girl's reply, though: "I'll go along if you want."

The man said something. The girl replied, "Well, don't be too long. Gary's asleep. You knew that, didn't you? He drank too damn much. Like always."

The man spoke again. When he stopped, the girl moved back into the kitchen and closed the door. The man stood at the gate for a moment, then opened it and came out along the path toward the cow stable. He's just out to get some exercise, Jodie thought. He'll turn at the cow stable and go back. He'll have to cross the fence to come on out here, and I reckon he won't do that. . . .

The man reached the stable, walking slowly, looking all around. He was bareheaded and in his shirt-sleeves. He stopped by the corner of the table, stood still and looked out across the fence toward the straw stack, then came on. Jodie began crawling backwards, wriggling on his belly. The man might stop at the fence, and he might not. Jodie knew he had to tell Easter the fellow was out there, coming this way. He knew the fellow could not see him, and guessed it was safe for him to slide down behind the stack. He slid down.

He landed right in front of Easter, and saw, before his feet hit the ground, that she was not dressed. She had taken off the pajama top and was naked except for bedroom slippers.

"Jodie!" she said in a sharp whisper. "Jodie, I'm— you shouldn't have come down now—"

"There's a guy coming this way from the house," he

23

told her, looking the other way. "It's Buzz. I heard a girl call him by his name. He was past the stable and heading for the field fence, the last I saw. I—I had to come down."

"Buzz—coming out here! Oh, my God, Jodie!"

"We'll have to hide in the stack, take the suitcase with us. We'll have to hurry."

"Jodie, I'm ashamed."

"I'll go first," he said, still not looking at her. He got down on his knees and began pushing and pulling at the straw. The straw was loose and dry. It took only a few seconds for him to open a tunnel into the side of the stack. As he did this, Easter made a hole in the straw, pushed the suitcase into it and covered it over. When Jodie backed away and looked at her again, she had on a skirt and blouse.

"Ruie and I always could wear each other's clothes," she whispered.

"Follow me," Jodie said, and dived back into the tunnel. In seconds, then, they were inside the stack and had filled the tunnel with straw behind them. They crouched on their knees side by side.

"Chances are," Jodie whispered, "Buzz didn't come any farther than the fence."

"Which is plenty close enough to suit me," Easter replied. "You ought to see that guy! Ugly—it gives me the crawlies just to remember how he looks."

"He could be looking for you," Jodie replied. "Maybe he doesn't believe you're in town visiting friends, like you said you heard your father tell him."

"What makes you say that, Jodie?"

"Oh, I don't know. The slow way he came through the back yard, maybe. The way he kept looking around. Do you really think they believed what your father told them about you?"

"Yes. Papa made it sound right. He told them Ruie was using my room. So that explained my bed being mussed. And Ruie has been using my room. I've been sharing it with her."

"I guess Buzz just came out for some fresh air, that's all," Jodie said, worriedly.

"I wonder where he is now?" Easter said apprehensively.

"Went back to the house, likely," Jodie told her.

She drew a deep breath. "Do you think he might hear us, whispering like this, if he's nearby out there?"

"No."

"I hope I put everything back in the suitcase."

"You did," Jodie said. "Don't worry." They were quiet for a few seconds, listening. Then Jodie said, "I'm going to lie down, try to relax." He lay down carefully on his belly, crossed his arms and rested his chin on them. Easter remained on her knees for a moment, then lay down close beside him.

"Golly, it's dark in here," she said.

"Yeah," he replied. "Were you ever inside a straw stack before?"

"Sure. Lots of times, when I was a little kid. Ruie and Walt and I used to play out here a lot. I guess Papa's been stacking his straw in this same spot for years. We used to dig tunnels and crawl through them, pretending we were bears. We made slides down the sides of the stack, too, and slid down them. Sometimes we'd wrestle and romp in the straw for hours. Papa didn't care. He wouldn't let us play around the hay stacks, though."

"Yeah," Jodie said. "It was the same way at my home. My paw always let me play in the straw, but he'd skite me out of the hay as quick as anything."

"Ruie said you were brought up on a farm, same as us—over by Stallerville, wasn't it?"

"You mean isn't it?" he said. "My folks still live on the home place."

"But you live in Stallerville now."

"Only since I've been working in the feed mill for your Uncle Rob."

"You live in the mill, don't you? Ruie said you did, said you have a room in the back, and have it fixed up real comfy."

"Oh, it's not much. Just a small room."

"Ruie said you played football something terrific. Maybe she was bragging. She said you're the best player Stallerville High ever had—said you won a scholarship to go to Greening U."

"We better not whisper so much," Jodie told her. "I don't think Buzz'll hear us, even if he's right outside. But if we keep on whispering, we won't hear him either. And I'd like to know if he's still around out there."

"Okay," she said meekly. "I'm sorry."

"You don't need to be," he replied quickly. "I like to talk with you."

"Do you, Jodie?"

"Sure. I'd like it a lot more if I wasn't so worried. Up there on the stack awhile ago, when I saw Buzz coming out this way, I thought I would scoot down and try to sneak up on him from behind and tackle him. Then I thought about the other one, Gary, and the two girls, and I thought if Buzz didn't go back to the house soon they'd get suspicious, and come out and look for him. But, Easter, I've got to do something to get Ruie and your paw and that girl away from those crooks, and I've got to do it before Walt gets here. I wish to God I could think of what it's going to be."

"What might they do if you tackled Buzz and knocked him out, and they got suspicious and looked for him and couldn't find him?" Easter asked.

"They'd get scared, that's what," Jodie said. "Yeah, they would probably get scared, and they would probably leave here in a hurry, and take Ruie and your paw and the Shetsher girl with them."

"Why would they take Ruie with them, Jodie?"

26

"Because they'd know if they left her behind she'd get word to the sheriff about them as soon as she could."

"Ruie wouldn't do that, Jodie. Ruie wouldn't do anything that'd get Papa into trouble."

"Well—well, Buzz and the others, they don't know that, I guess. They'd take her with them, all right, or maybe they'd kill her to shut her mouth."

"K-kill her?"

"Yes. They kidnapped a girl—do you think they'd hold off on killing, if it would save their hides?"

"'Do—do you—have you got a gun, Jodie?"

"No, of course not. Why would I have a gun? Why'd you ask?"

"Buzz and Gary've got guns. I saw their guns. They had them in their hands when they first came into the house. I guess if you'd tackled Buzz, like you thought you might, he'd have shot you pretty quick." Easter wriggled slightly as she spoke, and her hip rubbed against his, moved away quickly, then slowly moved back, rubbed against his again, and did not move away.

"I'm not afraid of them if they do have guns," he said. "Don't think I changed my mind about tackling Buzz because I'm afraid of him. I—"

She interrupted him. "I don't think that, Jodie."

"Well, please don't. I'm not afraid of anybody."

"I know. I know what you meant, too. We wouldn't want to do anything that might make them leave. At least, while they're here we can watch and listen, and maybe find out something about what's going on."

"Yeah," he mumbled. "We better keep quiet for a while and listen."

"Sure," she agreed. Then, a moment later, she asked. "Can you start a car without the ignition key—you know, wire it across or—or whatever it is they do?"

"Yes. Why?"

"Oh, nothing." She wriggled again, her thigh against his. Neither of them spoke for a few minutes. They did

27

not hear anything, except the small rustlings of the straw settling around them. Suddenly, Jodie asked, "How about the house, inside—how many rooms and hallways? Is there a back stairway?"

"No back stairway," Easter replied. "Four rooms upstairs, two on each side, with a narrow hallway in between. The stairs go up from the living room on the west wall of the house. The upstairs hall opens off them on the right. There's no hallway downstairs. Just three big rooms, living room, dining room, kitchen. There's no basement. There's a cellar house in the back yard. We call it the meat house."

"You said the girl was in one of the front bedrooms?"

"Yes. The first one from the top of the stairs. Walt's room."

"Would it be much trouble to climb onto the back porch roof?"

"No. I've done it more than once."

"Then I can," Jodie said.

"But you won't," Easter quickly replied. "It'd be too risky."

"I got to do something pretty soon," he said. "I don't figure on Ruie being in there with those kidnappers much longer, if I can help it."

"They won't bother her. She's Walt's sister, and Walt's their leader."

"Walt's not here," he said. "Maybe he won't ever be here. He might be in jail or dead by now. He might even be skinning out of the country with the ransom money, for all we know. If he doesn't show up at all, what do you think will happen to Ruie and your paw?"

"I—I don't know. You're scaring me, Jodie. Please don't scare me." She put her arm across his back, wriggled up tight against him. "I don't want to be afraid, Jodie."

"You have to be afraid, and so do I," he said. "We're in one hell of a fix. Your paw and Ruie and that girl

28

are in a hell of a lot worse fix than we are." He turned away from her and sat up, ignoring the feel of her hip, thigh, and arm. She clutched his shirt and held onto it.

"What are you going to do, Jodie?" Her whisper raked hard in her throat. Her hands on his chest were trembling.

"Crawl out of here, take a look around," he told her. "I figure Buzz is back in the house by now."

"But he might not be—"

"I'll be careful. I won't leave the stack until I'm sure he's not where he can see me."

She let go of his shirt and sat up beside him, letting her hand fall in his lap. "You're very much in love with Ruie, aren't you?" she asked.

"We're going to be married," he said, wonderingly.

She sighed softly. "Ruie was always the lucky one," she said. "Like when Uncle Rob wanted one of us to come to Stallerville and work for him. Papa picked Ruie to go. There's only a couple of years difference in our ages. I graduated from high school the same as she did. But she got to go."

"Did you want to go?" Jodie asked.

She chuckled. "Don't be silly, buddy boy. You think I enjoy living out here in the sticks? I'd leave here to-night if I had enough money, or if somebody would take me . . . well, not just *somebody,* but somebody I liked a lot."

He did not say anything. He tried to ignore the warmth of her hand in his lap, could not, and finally lifted her hand away.

"It gets crazy lonesome out here sometimes," she said. "It wasn't so bad with Ruie and Walt at home, but lately, with nobody here except Papa and me—my God! —I'm not going to stay here much longer. If I do, I'll go nuts."

"You leave, and what will your father do?"

"Go into Stallerville and make his home with Uncle

29

Rob," she replied. "Uncle Rob's been at him for a long time to sell the farm and move to town. But as long as Papa can have me here to keep house for him, he won't do it. He said so himself. So I'm leaving soon. Then he'll move into town. It'll be better for him in there. It'll be a lot better for me away from here."

She moved, and her hand fell into his lap again. He started to move it, then stopped as she said, "It wouldn't hurt none, I guess, if you'd hold me in your arms for a little while. I'm so worried and scared. I wish you would, Jodie. I know your arms around me would make me feel a lot better. And it wouldn't hurt none."

"Ruie and I are going to be married," he reminded her.

"Yes, I know," she said, sounding as though he had said something that hurt her feelings. "But I'm only asking you to hold me, comfort me a little bit." She paused, then started to cry. "I'm so worried and frightened!"

He put his arms around her. She sighed, but went on crying, softly, and snuggled up to him. She did not take her hand from his lap. Now and then it moved there, the fingers pulsing. He held her for a long time. She finally stopped crying, sighed and said, "Let's lie down, and you hold me, huh—huh, Jodie?"

3

"DID—did you ever—go all the way with a girl, Jodie?" Easter asked, as they lay straight out in the straw, bodies pressed tightly together, arms locked around each other.

Jodie started to reply, then stopped. They were quiet

for several seconds. At last he said, "That's a very personal question, Easter."

"I know," she murmured. "Like when you slid down the stack awhile ago and looked at me when you knew I was naked. That was a very personal thing, too."

"I had to slide down the stack. You know I did. Besides, you'd had time enough to dress. I didn't know you were naked."

"Well—" She was silent for a moment, hugging him hard. "Well," she finally said, "this is a very personal thing—you and I doing this, hugging and kissing. So I don't see why you won't tell me if you ever went all—all the way with a girl. I wouldn't tell on you. I wouldn't tell Ruie. If that's what you're worried about."

"No need for us to talk about me," he said.

She hugged him hard and kissed him on the mouth for a long time. Then, pulling the kiss apart, panting slightly, she said, "You and Ruie went all the way, more than once. I know it. You don't have to tell me, Jodie."

"Did Ruie tell you we did?" he asked, his voice stiffening.

"No. She wouldn't tell a thing like that on herself, silly. But I know it's true. Ruie's changed since she went away. She was a virgin when she left here to go to Stallerville and work for Uncle Rob. Now she's not. Don't ask how I know. I just do, that's all."

He was silent for a moment, remembering some of the things Ruie had told him about Easter. "Easter would be working for Uncle Rob instead of me," Ruie had once said, "only Papa doesn't trust her. I mean, he doesn't trust her to behave herself when she's around the fellows. She's better at figures than I am, and Uncle Rob wanted her more than he did me. But Papa was afraid to let her go, afraid she would get into trouble. You know—get in trouble with some fellow. Papa says she's too easy, a pushover for any fellow who might give her a try. Maybe he's right. I don't know."

And another time, when they were making love in his car, she had slapped him when he had sneaked his hand beneath her skirt and slipped it up her panty-leg, and angrily told him, "Don't ever do that again! I'm not going to be the kind of girl my sister is. I'm not going to have people talking about me, calling me a tramp. If you ever do that again, we're through. You hear me, Jodie? Through for good!"

But he had done it again the very same night, and the next night, and again, and again. And they were not through, not by a long shot. They were just beginning. They were in love. They were going to be married.

He said, slowly moving his hands up and down Easter's back, "Did you ever go all the way with a fellow, Easter?"

"Oh, oh!" she murmured, and softly laughed. "Now who's asking the very personal question?"

"Did you, Easter?"

She was silent for a time. He went on rubbing her slender back, slowly. His heart was pounding and he felt short of breath. His knees felt as if they might start to shake at any moment. He knew the feeling that was moving in on him; he had got acquainted with it the many times he had made love to Ruie.

Easter sighed and wriggled against him, wriggled up higher against him, so that her round buttocks came under his rubbing hands. "You think I have," she whispered thickly, her lips moving against his cheek. "Don't you, Jodie? You think I have. . . ."

"Have you, Easter?"

"You tell me first. Have you?"

"Yes."

"With Ruie?"

"I won't say. Let's not talk about Ruie . . . now."

32

"I'd bet it was with Ruie. I'd bet anything it was lots and lots of times with Ruie."

"Have you—have you done it with a fellow, Easter?"

She snuggled her face against his neck, kissed him there. "Yes."

He stopped rubbing and clutched her buttocks. She gave a small moan and struggled against him. "The fellow's in the army now," she whispered. "It was when I was seventeen. I—we thought we were in love, I guess. I know I did. I tried not to—to go all the way—let him go all the way ... I tried real hard. Honest. But I—I wanted to too much. Like—like now, Jodie . . ."

"I—I want to, too," he whispered "I want to a lot."

"I—I know."

"How?"

"I—I just do. I can—can feel, can't I?" She laughed thickly.

"How can we let ourselves act this way at a time like this?" he asked. "Those kidnappers here with that poor little frightened girl—your paw and Ruie in such awful danger—I just don't understand it."

"I—I don't understand it, either, Jodie. All I know is, I—I want you to do it to me."

He drew a long, hard breath. "A few minutes ago I wasn't even thinking of anything like this. Even when I saw you naked, and the starlight so bright all over you, I didn't get much excited or want to do anything. But now—Jesus! Now I feel that if I don't do it I'll go nuts or something. I—I guess I'm as hot as a firecracker, like my paw used to say about an old billygoat we had. That old billy was always sniffing and snorting and pawing the ground, and twisting his tail around. But a human being in his right mind ought to have better control of himself than that. But right now I guess I don't want to have better control. I guess I don't want to have any control at all."

33

"Do you want to take my clothes off, Jodie? There's only the skirt and blouse—"

He swore. "Oh, my God, I don't know!" He swore again, softly. "I don't know! I don't know! I don't know! I love Ruie. My God, Easter, we oughtn't to be acting like this. I'm going to marry Ruie. I'm going to be your brother-in-law. My God—"

"I'll never tell Ruie. Jodie, I'll never tell anyone. I know you love Ruie, and I know she loves you. I want you two to get married. Honest. I'll never tell."

"You just told me about yourself and that soldier. I don't know, Easter."

"But that was different. I'd never say anything that might spoil things between you and Ruie. Honest I wouldn't, Jodie honey."

"I—I guess you wouldn't," he mumbled. "But—but I—" He pushed her away and sat up, blinked around at the darkness.

He was panting, and so was she. He was moist all over his body with perspiration. "It's awful close in here," he whispered. "I wonder—I wonder if Buzz went back to the house. I guess I better crawl outside and take a look around."

She was hard against him then, hugging and kissing him. "Don't be afraid!" she pleaded. "Please, Jodie, don't be afraid. I won't tell Ruie a thing. Please, Jodie, make love to me!"

"I—I can't," he groaned. "I'm engaged to Ruie. I want to be true to Ruie. I love her and want to be true to her. Can't you understand that?"

"Yes. Yes, I understand. But—right now I want you and you want me. It won't hurt. Just once."

She was pulling up her blouse as she finished speaking. He could tell by her movements. She grabbed his hand and held it on her cool, shaking breasts. She unzipped her skirt, started to push his hand down under it. He jerked it away, scooted away from her. "No, by

34

God!" he whispered. "If my love for Ruie can't keep me from doing it to you, then it's no love at all. And it is love, all love, the way I feel about Ruie. I'd die for her. You let me alone now, Easter. I love Ruie. You let me alone."

She did not follow him. She said, "If I told you it was Ruie out there in the barn with Gary Summerfield, I guess you wouldn't be acting this way toward me now."

He went stiff in every muscle. "What?" he rasped, speaking aloud for the first time since they had crawled into the stack. "What did you say?"

"Well, that Gary—Gary Summerfield—he's no stranger around here," she answered hesitantly. "I didn't tell you that, did I? Well, he's not. His folks live three farms down the road from here. Gary's been around here all his life till he left a few months ago to take a construction job in Louisville. He and Ruie used to date a lot, too."

"All right, so they used to date a lot," he said, whispering again, but louder than before. "So what does that mean? You said it was Emma who was in the barn with him. That's what you said."

"I know what I said," she snapped, and this time she forgot herself and spoke out loud.

He gave a hard, troubled sigh. "But now you're going to change it, say it was Ruie, huh?"

"I didn't say I was."

He scooted back until his legs touched hers. He reached for her and his hand closed, remained for a moment on one of her breasts. He took it away, groped, found her arm, clutched it. "Well, was it Emma or was it Ruie?" he grated. "You better tell me—you better tell me the truth. You better! Or by God I'll—"

She tried to free her arm. "Stop, Jodie! You're hurting my arm. Stop now!"

"I'll hurt your neck if you don't tell me what I have

35

to know," he said. "Was it Emma or Ruie doing that with Gary in the barn?"

"I won't say. I don't have to say. Let go of me! Ask Ruie who it was. Ask her, you big simple bastard! And let go of me!"

"I can't ask her. I'm asking you. Who was it, Easter? Easter—"

"I won't say. I—"

He lunged forward and grabbed her by the shoulders and shoved her backwards, down in the straw. She clawed him, kicked, hit him, gasping hard little gasps and sobbing. He threw himself farther forward and straddled her thighs and got a fresh hold—a hand in her hair, a hand on her throat. "Now, by God," he said, "you tell me who was in the barn with that filthy scum, that dirty kidnapper, or—or I'll—I'll—"

He was choking her. She was struggling wildly, making gagging noises in her throat. It was like he knew what he was doing, yet did not know that he was doing it. It was somehow like remembering—like he had done it before and was only thinking about doing it now. The thought that he might have gone crazy flashed in his brain, stunning him for an instant. Then, suddenly, he was himself again—knew he had lost his temper, and was weakly glad that he had got it back again in time.

He let go of Easter's throat, got off of her and said, "I'm sorry. I've got one hell of a temper. I think I—I meant to kill you. Did I hurt you much?"

"N-no," she gasped, sobbing hard. "I—I'll be all right. You scared me almost to death. You—you're the strongest person who ever had hold of me in my whole life. Your hands were like iron."

"Was it Ruie in the barn with—with that Gary whatever his name is?" he asked. "Please tell me—tell me the truth if you know the truth. Was it Ruie?"

"I—I won't say. You'll have to find out from—"

36

He cut her off. "You're a mean little no-good bitch," he said calmly. "I guess you know that." He got up on his knees, turning away from her.

"What are you going to do?" she asked.

"What you told me to do," he replied. "Ask Ruie if she was in the barn with Gary awhile ago."

"But—but you can't! You go in the house, and Buzz or Gary will kill you!"

"I've got to know if Ruie was doing that with Gary," he said. "Right now I don't give a damn about anything else. I've got to know, and I'm going to find out, one way or another."

He began tunneling in the straw, crawling and tunneling. "Wait!" Easter said. "Please wait. Please don't go in the house. I'll tell you what you want to know. I'll tell you the truth this time."

He stopped clawing the straw, got up straight on his knees, and waited. "All right," he said. "Go on, tell me. Tell me the truth."

He heard her crawling toward him. Then he heard something else. Easter heard it, too, and stopped crawling. It was a sudden sound, and soon ended. Neither of them spoke until they heard it again. Then Easter said, in a shaking whisper, "That's Aggie calling Buzz. He must still be outside somewhere."

Jodie started to say, "I wonder where he is?" But he did not say it; for just then a man's voice spoke up. It was Buzz's voice. He was right here, right outside the stack, and he was saying, "I'm over here, Aggie. By the straw stack. Come on over. I just found something interesting—a big carving knife and a woman's pajama top. Come on over. Help me look around here in the straw. Could be somebody's here, maybe hiding inside the stack."

Jodie saw in his mind how it was—Buzz waiting by the stack for Aggie, the carving knife and Easter's pajama top in his hands; Aggie hurrying out from the house to join him. He wondered what he would do now if he were in Buzz's place, and instantly decided he would do some searching, search the stack, on it, inside it, and all around.

He thought, I guess he doesn't believe now that Easter is off visiting friends, like her father said. I guess he figures she was here when he and his friends arrived with the girl, is still here, hiding, or on her way to the nearest telephone to call the law. I guess he'll run now, him and his friends, and take the Shetsher girl with them. Or maybe they won't take her with them. Maybe they'll kill her, kill Ruie. . . . His pores seemed to sprout ice.

After Buzz called to Aggie there had been only silence; but now there was a small rustling, as Easter moved close to Jodie, put her arms around him, whispered, "Oh, Jodie, I made an awful mistake! I—I was sure I put the knife and my pajama top in Ruie's suitcase, but I didn't." Her lips touched his ear, coldly trembled against it. "Oh, Jodie, I'm sorry!"

He did not say anything. He was not angry with her now, only concerned for her safety, for Ruie's safety, for his, for Mr. Danson's, and the kidnapped girl's. He tried to decide what was best to do, and the only thing that seemed right was for him to go out there, try to knock Buzz senseless, tie him up.

But right now was a bad time for that, with Aggie around to help Buzz, or to fetch Gary to help him. He started to ask Easter if she thought she could handle Aggie if he went out and tackled Buzz. But just then Aggie said, "This pajama top matches the bottoms we found in that Easter's room. That old man lied. That girl ain't in town visiting, like he said. I'd bet anything she heard us coming and skinned out of the house, and

38

is right now hiding around here somewhere. Maybe inside this straw stack."

Buzz gave a flat laugh. "Figure if she had this pajama top on she'd leave it on," he said. "Figure she wouldn't want to crawl into the stack naked."

"Don't be so dumb," Aggie replied. "She probably snatched up a dress or something as she run out of the house, came on out here and changed to it. She's around here, Buzz. I feel positive she is. She wouldn't go for the law, when her brother and father are in this as deep as anybody. Right now she's probably hiding and waiting for a chance to get her father and sister away from us."

"You forgetting this knife?" Buzz asked. "I found it wrapped up in the pajama top. You figure she snatched it up when she ran out of the house, or what?"

"The knife don't interest me," Aggie said. "She had it. She got it somewhere and brought it out here. Maybe she thought she would need it to protect herself, and hid it where she could get at it easy. Or maybe she got hold of a gun after getting the knife, and decided she could do without the knife. I don't know. I only know she's around here somewhere, close. I feel it in my bones that she is. And she's got to be found; we've got to find her. We don't, we're going to be in bad trouble, if we ain't already."

"I wish to hell Walt'd show," Buzz grumbled. "He should have been here by now. You think he got the money and skinned out of the country? You think he's double-crossed us, Aggie?"

"No," Aggie replied.

And Easter whispered in Jodie's ear, "He won't show. Not if he got the ransom. He'd take a chance on getting killed before he'd divide the money with the others. She doesn't know how selfish he is, that's all."

Jodie was listening to Buzz and did not reply.

"We better look around here some," Buzz said. "Might be we'll find something else."

There were sounds of straw being pawed, pushed about. Easter sighed and settled down off her knees, against Jodie. He took his arm from around her, but she continued to embrace him. "I'm scared," she said once, then was quiet.

"They'll find the suitcase, likely," Jodie told her, bending and putting his lips against her cheek. "If they do, they'll likely come on in here, looking. You think you can handle Aggie, if they find us and I have to jump Buzz?"

Easter moved her face up and down against his. "Yes. The way I feel I could take care of two like her."

They heard Buzz grunt, then exclaim, "Here's something! Feels like a—box. Give me the flashlight."

"He found it," Jodie whispered. "And they got a flashlight."

"A—a box?" Aggie said, excitedly. "You sure?"

"It's a suitcase!"

"A—a suitcase, Buzz!"

"Yeah."

A moment later the rustling sounds ceased, and Jodie guessed the contents of the suitcase were being examined. They can't know I'm here, he thought. The suitcase and what's in it can't tell them that. They'll probably decide the suitcase is Easter's. But if something in it shows it's Ruie's, I wonder what they'll think. . . .

"All girl's stuff, except the pipe and tobacco pouch," Aggie said, suddenly. "Easter's stuff. She hid it out here. Walt said she was fed up with living here, being a housekeeper for the old man. Remember, Buzz?"

"No. I didn't hear him say it."

"Well, he said it. Gary heard him. And that's why she stashed this stuff out here. She's planning to skin out and leave the old man. I'm sure glad you found it. Now we know she's still here. She wouldn't leave with-

40

out this stuff—an expensive skirt and blouse, a good, almost new pair of shoes. Easter's still here, okay. Maybe right here, hiding so close that she's hearing every word we say."

"You think she's inside the stack?"

"Yes, I do. I found a place where the straw is all loose, like it just now settled back where someone made a tunnel, crawling into it. I'd bet she's in the stack, or was in it. She could easy have sneaked out on the other side while we've been yakking."

"Give me the flash," Buzz said.

"What're you going to do?" Aggie asked, her voice sharpening with concern.

"Crawl into the stack and get her if she's in there," Buzz replied.

"And maybe get your brains blowed out? My God, Buzz, but you're thick between the ears. Easter had a knife and didn't hold on to it. So it's a good bet she found a better weapon—a gun."

"I doubt it. Farmers don't keep guns around much."

"Walt lived here, don't forget," Aggie replied. "He probably left a gun or two lying around when he went away."

"Okay," Buzz said impatiently. "She's got a gun. So what do we do, hang around here till she starves to death?"

"No," Aggie replied, "we burn her out—or burn her up. You got your cigarette lighter with you?"

"Yes." Buzz paused and there was a moment of silence. "My God, Aggie!" he finally exclaimed. "My God. Do you know what you just said? Do you know how straw burns when it's dry like this straw is?"

"Sure I do. Give me your cigarette lighter."

"The crazy bitch is going to set the stack on fire!" Easter gasped, hugging Jodie harder—so hard it became difficult for him to breathe. "Oh, Jodie, what can we do?"

He pulled and pushed her arms from around him. "You go out there," he said. "Tell them you're coming out. Right now. Tell them. While you're tunneling out this side of the stack, I'll be tunneling out the other side. They won't do anything to you right off. They'll only talk for a while. You keep them talking as long as you can, keep them interested in you. I'll sneak around the stack and clobber Buzz. When I do, you tackle Aggie. Okay?"

"I—I don't know . . ."

"You afraid of her?"

"No. I—I—that Buzz—he gives me the crawlies just to look at him."

"Don't worry about Buzz. Aggie's your project. Go ahead. Tell them you're coming out."

He felt her stiffen, as if she was readying herself to cry out. Then he heard Buzz ask, "How about the neighbors?"

In the next moment Easter gasped and went taut against him.

"There ain't any close neighbors," Aggie replied. "We don't have to worry about them. Gary said so, and he ought to know."

"Lots of neighbors close enough to see this straw stack burning if you set it on fire," Buzz said.

Silence followed this remark. Then, finally, Aggie said, "I guess you got something there. I guess people would see the fire, all right, and come running."

"You betcha they would," Buzz said.

"Well—well, we'll just have to crawl in there and get her, if she's there to be got," Aggie said, resignedly.

"Not both of us," Buzz said. "One of us needs to be out here to stop her if she comes pawing out of there and tries to run. I'll go inside."

"Okay."

"Here's my gun," Buzz said. "If there's any shooting in the stack you give a yell. If I don't answer, set the

42

stack on fire and shoot little Easter full of holes when she comes out. Here—give me that knife."

Buzz said this last in a loud voice. Jodie told Easter, "He wanted you to be sure and hear. He's coming in. I don't want to fight him in here. Let's climb up through the straw. Maybe we can give him the slip."

"He—he'll hear us," Easter whispered jerkily.

"Not the noise he's making he won't. Come on. Start climbing. Straight up. Whatever happens, we'll have the advantage of them once we're on top of the stack."

Minutes later, long before Buzz gave up searching in the straw, they were lying on top of the stack, hip to hip, on their bellies, looking down. They saw Buzz burrow backwards from the stack, stand up in the bright starlight, brush bits of straw off his clothing, heard him swear, then mumble complainingly.

"She was in there, sure enough," he said. "I found the place where she nested in. The straw was packed down and still warm. But she's not in there now. She can't be. I made a honeycomb of the damn place. And I'm damn near pooped from doing it."

"She sneaked out while we were talking," Aggie said. "But she's still around. The way things are, I bet she couldn't be hauled away from here with a team of horses." She squatted, facing the stack, and reached out with both hands into the stack's shadow. "We'll find her, don't worry."

She was pulling something toward her. It was the suitcase. When it appeared from the shadow, Easter gave a small, angry gasp.

"We going to look for her right away, or what?" Buzz asked.

"In the morning we'll look for her," Aggie replied. "She can't give us the slip then, in daylight."

"Maybe when we tell Gary and Emma about this, they won't want to wait till daylight to do something about her."

Aggie gave a lewd laugh. "Gary knows her good," she said, opening the suitcase and pawing its contents. "He used to run around with her. Remember how disappointed he acted when the old man said she wasn't here?"

"He didn't seem disappointed to me."

"Well, he was," Aggie said. "Could be he'll want to look for her tonight—by himself. He's got ideas about her, all right."

"What are you after in there, Aggie?"

"These," Aggie said, holding up a bra and panties. "Ain't they cute? My size, too. There's a skirt here I like, too. And I hope these shoes fit me." She put down the bra and panties and picked up a pair of shoes. Jodie recognized them as Ruie's most expensive, most cherished ones. He thought, She meant to wear them back to Stallerville. And that no-good slut pawing over her clothes like that . . . messing around with her underthings . . .

Easter planted her lips against his ear, started to whisper something, then gave a little gasp, looking down. Jodie looked down, too. Easter said, "Goddamn her, she's stealing Ruie's clothes!"

Aggie had put the shoes back in the suitcase. She was standing up, taking off her clothes. Buzz was staring at her. Jodie and Easter stared at her. She took off every stitch, stooped and got Ruie's panties and bra from the suitcase, handed the panties to Buzz to hold, then put on the bra.

Buzz laughed thickly, slapped her on the buttocks as she wriggled, fastening the bra. She squirmed. She laughed, finished hooking the bra and reached for the panties. Buzz wadded them up and put them in his pants pocket.

Aggie said, "Aw, Buzzie. Give them to me."

"Huh-uh," he muttered. He laughed and grabbed her.

"Aw, Buzzie, not now, not again so soon," Aggie said.

"Soon?" he muttered, holding her close and racing his hands up and down her back, fingers clutching, pinching, rubbing. "What do you call soon? It was two hours or more ago, and then it was only once. This man of yours is a real man, baby."

"But I want to try on these nice clothes. I'm going to keep them, Buzz. All of them. Why don't you take the pipe and tobacco pouch?"

He laughed thickly and unfastened her bra. "Me smoke a pipe?" He dropped the bra on top of the stuff in the suitcase, pulled Aggie over near the stack and began kicking straw from the stack, spreading it around on the ground. He did not let go of her once, but kept feeling of her, his big hands hopping here, there, clutching, pinching, rubbing. His hands reminded Jodie of big rats, playing.

Aggie was slightly resistant, then passive, then she became interested. They kissed, for a long time. Buzz's hands went on racing. Aggie was hugging him now, moaning low in her throat as they kissed.

Jodie glanced at Easter. Easter was staring at the lovers, her eyes wide, her mouth slightly open. She was clutching the straw with both hands.

Suddenly, Buzz picked Aggie up, held her in his arms, kissed her on the belly, ran his mouth up and kissed her between her shaking breasts. Aggie moaned and seemed to shudder, and Buzz dropped down, on to his knees on the bed of straw he had made with his feet.

He laid Aggie down on the straw on her back. Jodie glanced at Easter again, and found her staring at him. As their eyes met, she wriggled around, on to her side, and put her arms around him.

"Oh, Jesus," she sighed, "how can I stand it? Oh, Jesus, how can I? I—I feel like I'm going to smother to death. Oh, Jodie, hon! Oh, Jodie, sweet!" She pushed her face beneath his chin and kissed him on the neck. "Oh, Jodie, let's . . . Let's! Please, Jodie!" She was hugging him,

45

tugging at him, trying to turn him off his belly. He would not let her. She threw one leg across his thighs, wriggled the other leg underneath, sighed, said, "Oh, damn you! Damn you!" She tugged at him again. He would not be moved. She hugged him with legs and arms, fiercely. "How can you stand it?" she asked. "Are you all ice and iron or what? Just look what they're doing down there! Oh, my God! How can you stand it?"

"You're a mean little bitch," he said. "You won't tell me if it was Ruie in the barn with Gary. I guess that's why I'm all ice and iron, if I am. I just don't like you. I just don't like you worth a nickel, that's all."

"It—it wasn't Ruie in the barn," Easter gasped. "It wasn't. It was that other girl, Emma. It wasn't Ruie, Jodie."

"That's what you say now—"

"My God, you're going to marry Ruie and you don't trust her enough not to believe she was making monkey business in the barn with Gary Summerfield. My God! But it wasn't Ruie with Gary. It was that Emma."

"You could have told me so before."

"I—I thought if I made you distrust Ruie that you might—might feel more easy in your mind about making love to me."

He turned over. She sighed, smiled, wriggled against him hard. He hugged her close. She still had her legs around his thighs. Suddenly she stopped hugging him. In the next second her hands were between them, her fingers pulling at his belt, unbuckling it . . .

4

"I'M in love with Ruie and she's in love with me," Jodie whispered. "We're going to be husband and wife soon.

I—I don't want anything like this, like what you and I are getting into—between us. So—so, Easter, I—I'm not going to . . . I'm not, Easter. I mean it."

She was struggling to get beneath him, pulling at him, embracing and kissing and tugging at him. She was working at it without making too much noise, but she was working at it hard. Jodie was wet with perspiration, but Easter was drenched with it. Having her at him like this, like a wild animal about to devour him, almost, was a new experience. He had considered Ruie a very passionate girl, but now . . . He did not know why he did not go ahead and satisfy her, and himself. He certainly craved to be satisfied. He just did not know why. It was like Ruie was all inside him, all outside him, holding him back. But that was silly. For a moment, as Easter kissed him, hot wet lips jerking at his, hot wet tongue sliding in and out between his lips, he thought he would let himself go. His hands closed on her writhing body, just below the roll of her pulled-high skirt, and he lifted himself up slightly, and over.

"Oh!" she gasped. "Oh, Jodie!"

Then, right then, the sounds below them stopped.

Jodie went rigid, listening. So did Easter. A moment passed. Another. Far off in the night an owl was chortling. Nearer, everywhere all around, insects were buzzing, clicking, chirruping. They heard only these things, nothing else, until Buzz said, "If I'd go get that Ruie and fetch her out here and do something to her that'd make her squall and beg, maybe that sister of hers would show herself, if she's around and happened to hear. I mean, if she thought I'd kill that Ruie if she didn't show, she'd show. What do you think, Aggie?"

Aggie did not answer right away, and Easter, looking up at Jodie, her face wet, bright and angry in the starlight, filled the interval with a slow, bitter oath. "You waited too long, you cold-meated bastard," she whispered. "We could have had our fun while they were having theirs and they wouldn't have heard. But you waited too long, and I'll get—I'll get you good—I'll get good'n hunk with you, you'll see."

He got off her slowly, carefully, and lay down on his belly. "Did you hear what Buzz said?" he asked. 'He's thinking of fetching Ruie out here and torturing her. I'm going to kill him. You hear! I'm going to kill him!"

"You ain't going to do nothing," Easter replied, her whisper heavy with disgust. "You ain't nothing but a big bag of wind. A fellow who'd treat a girl like you treated me just now, ain't got any guts. And you talk about killing somebody. You ain't even got the nerve to kill a damn little ol' ant. You're a weary willie if I ever met one."

He tried not to hear her, tried not to know what she said.

She went quiet when Aggie's voice said, "It might work. Depends on how much Easter cares about Ruie. But it wouldn't hurt to try it. You ain't figuring on really mussing Ruie up, are you? You ain't forgot she's Walt's sister."

"No, I ain't forgot," Buzz replied. "I think Gary better take care of it. He can sling the bull better'n me. He knows Walt better'n me, too. He'll know just how far he can go with Ruie."

"Yeah," Aggie replied. "Yeah, if I was you I'd let Gary handle it. You ready to go to the house now?"

"Yeah. Say, those clothes fit you all right. Look like they were made for you! You look real snazzy, baby."

Aggie laughed softly, proudly. "They're really good. Expensive. I'm surprised a dirt farmer's daughter like Easter would own such fine things. I'm glad she did own them, though."

Buzz chuckled. "I reckon you are so," he said.

Jodie and Easter stood on their knees and watched Buzz and Aggie go to the house. Aggie was wearing Ruie's best outfit, right down to the shoes, and carrying

48

Ruie's suitcase. When they disappeared for a moment behind the meat house, Easter swore a hard oath. She said, "The damn dirty little whore! I only hope I get a chance at her. I do, I'll claw her eyes out. The rotten little thief!"

"When she goes in the house dressed like that, carrying the suitcase," Jodie muttered, "Ruie'll know I'm here, but she won't know if I'm alive or dead. Likely she'll think the worst, that I'm dead or bad hurt. 'Cause she'll know I wouldn't give up the suitcase without a fight. But maybe Buzz or Aggie'll tell how they came by the suitcase. Maybe they will. If they do, then Ruie won't worry so much."

Easter made a slushy, smacking sound with her lips. "Ruie—Ruie—Ruie!" she said. "Is she all you ever think about, talk about? By God, I don't see where she's such a great prize. She never had a fellow in her life I couldn't take away from her, and didn't."

"Did you take Gary Summerfield from her?"

"No. She never had him. They went around together some, but they never went together steady. Gary used to be stuck on me, though."

"Do you like him?"

"Yes."

"Enough to be on his side when I tangle with him?"

She gave a slow, mocking laugh. "When you tangle with him, my foot! You ain't going to tangle with Gary. He'd beat your head off. You ain't going to tangle with anybody. You're a coward."

"Gary fetches Ruie out here, you'll see how I'm a coward," he said.

She laughed again. "You know something, Jodie—"

"I know a few things. I know enough to be true to the girl who's going to be a mother to my children."

"Jodie, I'm going to make you do it to me," Easter said, and laughed. "I am. I'm going to make you do it

49

to me. I'm going to make you want to, and I'm going to make you do it."

"I never heard of a girl raping a fellow," he said.

She laughed once more. "I didn't notice Buzz and Aggie going into the house," she said.

"I did. They went in by the kitchen door, while you were calling me a coward."

"Oh—Jodie—"

"Yeah."

"If you do get up enough nerve to tackle Gary, I won't be on his side. My God, you don't think I'd help out a dirty kidnapper, do you?"

"I don't know what I think of you," he replied, not looking at her. "Sneaking up on me in the dark, and nothing on but your pajama top, and holding a knife to my back—acting the way you have, so crazy to make love, and those kidnappers and the little girl they stole in your house, and Ruie and your father in awful danger—I don't understand how you could even so much as think of making love under such circumstances." He looked at her suddenly, shook his head, frowning. "I never did meet anybody like you. I guess you're a little bit nutty. And I guess you better lay off of me. I'm not having any of you no matter what you do, and that's all there is to it."

She was watching him, thoughtfully. When he stopped, she laughed softly. "You've having some of me, all right," she said. "You're going to beg for some of me before long. You'll see."

He dropped on all fours and crawled over to the edge of the stack, looking toward the house. "Gary's not fetching Ruie out here very fast," he said.

"Maybe he doesn't think Buzz's idea was much," Easter replied. "Or maybe he's too drunk to fetch her out. He was drinking in the barn before you got here. So was Emma."

"He drink a lot?"

"He used to when he was staying at home. I don't know much about him now. He's been away from here for a long time, following construction work all over the country."

"He's real tough, huh?"

"Yeah. He's real tough. He's got a gun, too. Like I said, he and Buzz both have guns."

"Could be Ruie's putting up a fight," Jodie said. He turned around, making ready to slide down off the stack.

"What are you going to do?" Easter crawled over to where he was, watching him wonderingly.

"I'm going to see what's going on in the house," he said.

"And get your brains blowed out—"

"They're my brains." He twisted himself and slid down the stack, braking his movement by digging into the straw with hands and feet. Easter said something he did not catch, then slid down after him.

They looked into each other's eyes for a moment, she pushing the tail of her blouse down inside the waistband of her skirt.

Her hair was mussed, all wild. Her eyes seemed too bright, dark silver with the starlight in them.

He said, "You better stay here. It's best if I know where to find you. No telling what'll happen."

She nodded. "I'm as scared and worried over all this as you are, maybe more," she said. "I know I shouldn't have acted like I did. But—but—well, I'm the way I am. I'm a little bit nutty, maybe . . . like you said. I don't want you to be sore at me, Jodie."

"You stay here. Hide if you see Gary and Ruie coming this way—if you see any of them coming this way."

"All right, Jodie."

"This is an awful dangerous and an awful bad thing that's happening," he said.

She nodded. "I know."

He turned quickly and walked away, not looking back.

It took less than a minute to reach the house. He paused in the shadow of a tree in the back yard, waited a few seconds—saw no one, heard no one. He moved on, paused again on the back porch. It was quiet here. He got the idea he was being watched, and a shiver went up and down his back. Once he heard someone laugh inside the house—a man. He guessed it was Buzz.

He moved about a little, taking hold of the porch posts and shoving, hard. He tested them all. He guessed any one of them would support his weight. He finally chose the middle one, held onto it and climbed up on the banister. He crouched there a moment, listening.

He could hear voices inside the house, but indistinctly, and could not even guess whose they were. He could not understand anything that was being said. Once someone said "Buzz" especially loud, then a girl laughed.

He thought they seemed unworried, and wondered if Ruie had seen her clothes on Aggie and claimed them, and they were no longer worried about Easter being out here, spying on them.

"But if Ruie claimed her clothes," he whispered, "she would have to explain how they came to be out in the straw stack. Surely, she wouldn't tell them I was here. And she wouldn't be able to give a sensible reason for hiding them in the straw stack herself." He waggled his head, puzzled, then took hold of the porch eaves with both hands and wrapped his legs around the post.

It was not difficult, climbing up onto the porch roof. The roof slanted only slightly, and it was no chore to walk over to the house wall. There were two windows here. One of them opened on Easter's bedroom, he knew. He guessed it was the one on his left, and went to it, crouched and walking on tiptoe.

He was surprised to find the window unlocked. He raised it slowly, carefully, and saw it did not have a

52

lock. The room he climbed down into was dark. He saw a thread of yellow light down low, guessed it came from the hallway, through the crack under the door. He went to it, tense, listening.

He could still hear the voices, but less distinctly than when he was on the porch. He stood by the door for a long moment, then tried the knob. It turned without a sound. The door was not locked. He opened it a small crack and looked out into a narrow, carpeted hallway. He could hear the voices plainly now. A girl was laughing, like she was making fun of someone. A man spoke. It was Gary's voice. Jodie recognized it instantly.

"Easter won't be calling the law, she wouldn't turn her own pappy in. She's just scared. She'll likely hide around out there for a while, then come on in here of her own accord. We don't need to worry none about her."

"Them ain't Easter's duds," a man's voice replied. "I reckon I ought to know my own daughter's duds, and them ain't Easter's. And Easter ain't here. She's off visiting, like I said before. I got the word from Walt. I knowed you was coming here with the girl. So I sent Easter off to visit in town. You don't have to believe me. But it's the truth, anyway. And that suitcase, I never seen it before in my life."

Jodie knew he had just heard Jason Danson, and shook his head. The old man was a very convincing liar, and he did not sound intimidated or much distressed, either. Jodie opened the door a little wider, looked out, up and down the hall. An oil lamp, flame turned low, bracketed the wall opposite Jodie, furnished the light here. The door beside it was open. The room beyond the door was dark.

"Walt's room," Jodie told himself, remembering what Easter had said about the arrangement of the rooms up here. "The girl's in there if they didn't move her . . ."

He opened the door wide enough to pass through it,

53

then paused, listening. Aggie was talking. Another girl laughed. The voice was not Ruie's, so he guessed it was Emma's. He heard Buzz say something, but did not understand him; then Gary said something, also unintelligible, and laughed. They were all downstairs; he had heard them all, save Ruie and the Shetsher girl. He guessed Ruie was downstairs, too. She just was not talking, that was all.

He stepped out into the hall, stood still a moment, then crossed over and entered Walt's room. He saw the girl as soon as he passed through the door—saw her in near darkness, lying on the bed, back to him, huddled. He went to her, saying in a whisper, "I'm Jodie Saylem, Ruie's boy friend. I'm here to help you. Please don't speak out loud."

She jerked her head around, looked up over her shoulder. "You—you know what happened, everything?" she whispered.

"Yes." He saw she was tied, hands behind her, feet tied together at the ankles. He saw, too, that she was not altogether as Easter had described her—not so young, not so frail. He guessed her age at around twenty. She looked quite healthy, and very pretty. He thought, Maybe she'll look more like Easter said in the light. But he did not think so; he thought she would be even prettier when clearly seen.

He began untying the many knots in the cords that bound her wrists together. "I climbed onto the roof of the back porch and got into the room across the hall through a window," he told her, whispering with his mouth close to her ear. "We'll go out that way. You—you're all right, aren't you? They didn't hurt you or anything—"

"I'm all right," she replied. "I'm scared, is all. They —they got me last night. I was swimming in our pool— it's private and all—there's a high iron picket fence around our property. They came out of the shrubbery

54

beside the pool and grabbed me when I came out to take a dive. I—I was so frightened I—I fainted. Later, when I came to, I was sick. I—I threw up, and—"

"Were you swimming alone?" he interrupted.

"Yes."

"Don't talk any more," he told her. Then, more to himself than to her, "I wish I had a knife."

"There were three of them, but one of them didn't make the trip here with us. The other two picked up those—those girls in Maysville."

"Kentucky?"

"Yes."

"Don't say anything else till we get out of here," he told her.

He heard them coming as he untied the last knot. The girl shook her hands free, rubbed them together, rubbed her face with them, and sat up. At first he was not sure who was on the stairs; then he knew them as he heard Buzz insist, "The old man's lying. Easter's right here on the farm. I got a plan that'll prove she is. I'll tell you about it as soon as we look in on the girl."

"Easter ain't no problem," Gary's voice replied. "She won't give us away. I know her good. She's as crooked as Walt."

The Shetsher girl clutched at Jodie's arm. "Leave!" she husked. "Hurry! Oh, please!"

"Lie down like you were, put your hands behind you," he told her. "I'll put the cords back. Maybe they won't notice they're untied. I'll be in the room across the hall. I'll be back as soon as they leave."

"Oh, hurry."

They were in the hall by the time he reached the door. He took a quick, guarded look around the jamb; and there they were, moving toward him—two big, formidable men, no more than a step and a jump way. He turned back, heard the girl gasp in despair.

55

He would have to find a place to hide, or fight them here. "Is there a wardrobe?" he whispered, moving around the foot of the bed.

"Yes," the girl said. "The door's right in front of you."

He found the door, clutched and rolled the knob.

"Did you find it?" The girl's whisper was sharp, frantic.

"Yes," he said. "Don't worry. We'll be okay. They won't take a good look. Just don't move your hands."

"I already have," she panted. "The cords fell off my wrists and I—I can't put them back!"

He pulled on the knob. Nothing happened. He rolled it again, pulled on it again. Nothing happened. "My God!" he whispered. "The door won't open!"

The starlight had let Easter watch Jodie enter the house through her bedroom window. She stood leaning deep in the straw, against the straw stack, and watched the house, waiting for him to come out of it the way he had gone in. If he had good luck, the Shetsher girl and Ruie would come out with him. She hoped he would not have good luck, hoped he would be forced to leave the house as he had entered it, alone. She did not want Ruie out here, messing things up. She did not want the Shetsher girl set free just yet, either. She had her own ideas as to what should be done about the Shetsher girl, and she hoped to have a hand in the doing of it.

"I've been dog poor all my life," she told herself. "I've never had decent clothes, a decent place to live. I don't have any decent friends, just ignorant clods . . . I'm sick and tired of not having a bathroom, of having to sleep on a straw tick . . . of having to use a privy . . . I've been dog poor all my life, but by God I ain't always and forever going to be . . . Not if I can do anything to prevent it. And now's my chance—if that damn cheating, lying brute of a brother of mine did what I think he's already done—skinned to the hell and gone plumb out of the country with the ransom money."

She drew a long, deep breath, let it out slowly, thinking of Jodie, wishing he was different, not so dumb. "All honest folks are stupid," she told herself. "Like that angel-faced sister of mine—stupid. But maybe I can use him. Maybe I can make the stupid fool do what I want."

She watched the house and looked all around, listening deeply; but most of the time she watched her bedroom window. She was watching it when she heard the hens in the henhouse begin making those hushed, creepy, peepy noises they always made when there was an owl, a weasel, or some other bloodthirsty varmint bothering around the coop.

The henhouse stood on her left, a long stone's throw from the house. She could not see it without moving and looking around the straw. And she did not want to move, lest she miss seeing Jodie when he left the house. So she only listened, telling herself, "A damn ol' weasel sniffling around in the wall cracks. I don't figure he can get in. If he does, there'll be a sight more racket from the hens than there is now."

The hens kept on complaining, their little cries becoming louder and louder. Suddenly one of them began to cackle. Easter left the straw stack then, moved around it until she could see the henhouse, then stopped dead still, stood for a moment, then slowly went into a squat. "God'l mighty!" she gasped.

The henhouse door was opening. No one was by it, on the outside. It was opening very slowly. Then it was wide open and a man was stepping through it, a tall, thick-bodied man, wearing loose dark coveralls and a slouch hat. The hat was pulled low over his eyes. "Chicken thief!" Easter whispered. "And here tonight of all nights! God'l' mighty!"

The man closed the door, turned, stood up straight

57

and peered all around. He was in the shadow of the henhouse and she could not see him clearly. "But he ain't got nothing in his hands," she told herself wonder-ingly. "No bag or nothing . . . Now what was he doing in our henhouse if he wasn't stealing chickens, I'd like to know?"

She gulped, startled, almost choked on saliva, as the man moved out in a fast walk directly toward her. A moment later she went forward from her squatting posi-tion, onto all fours, and began slowly crawling back around the straw stack.

She had no idea who the man was. In such loose coveralls and with his hat pulled down like that, he could have been her father and she would not have recognized him. She burrowed a little way into the stack, turned, peeked out.

She could not see him, but she could hear him—hear his footsteps, and he was very near, still moving swiftly toward her.

Panic seized her. Her kness began to knock together. He had seen her, was coming for her—she felt certain he knew where she was. She thought of burrowing deep inside the stack, then changed her mind. "I better run," she told herself. "I better sneak and get the stack be-tween him and me, then run."

She crawled forward, then to her left, keeping close in against the stack. She could not hear him while she was crawling. She stopped after moving a few feet, and listened. She did not hear a thing. He was standing still, or sneaking along. She did not hear a thing.

"Oh, sweet Jesus," she whispered. She jumped up and ran, around the stack, then straight toward the house.

She did not look back, not once, until she was pass-ing by the meat house, racing in its shadow. But she knew he was chasing her. She just felt it. At the corner of the meat house, she whipped her head around, and there he was, already with her in the building's shadow.

58

He was practically reaching for her. She could hear his breaths, loud and short. A vision of the butcher's tools hanging inside the meat house, on the wall, jumped up in her mind. The big bone cleaver hanging there—

She pivoted as she cleared the corner, darted to her left. In the next moment she was past the door, closing it. The lock was on the outside, a big bolt-and-keeper affair. There was no lock inside. There was no means of fastening the door. How dark it was! She streaked around the big meat block, felt, snatched the bone cleaver off its hook. She whirled about.

What happened then made her blood seem to stop, to curdle all along her veins. It was not anything much, really—only a sound, a rasping and a thocking—a sound telling her that the bolt on the door had been shoved hard into its keeper—a sound telling her the door was locked, that she was here to stay until someone let her out.

"Oh, sweet Jesus!" she gasped, clutching the bone cleaver, crouching forward in the tarry darkness. "He locked me in! The bastard locked me in! Now why did he do that? He's coming back. He locked me in for safe keeping. He's got something more important than me to attend to right now, but he's coming back when he finishes with it, whatever it is. He's coming back, and what will he do to me then—what will he do to me then?"

5

A flashlight was turned on: Buzz turned it on. Its beam streaked out, spotted the Shetsher girl's huddled figure, then racked over the bed, here, there, all around. "Looks okay here," Buzz said. He stopped near the middle of

59

the room. Gary walked over to the bed. He looked down at the girl. "Let's go back downstairs," Buzz said.

"Yeah, in a sec," Gary answered. He put out a hand, laid it on the girl's hip. "You okay, bathing beauty?" he asked.

"Take your filthy hand off me," the girl said, not moving. Her back was to him. She wore a kimona, pink with big black dots. It was old and worn. She did not seem to have anything on under it. Her feet were bare. Her hair was dark rust-red, and mussed, and just the perfect length for an extra long pony tail. Gary did not take his hand off her.

"You want anything?" he inquired. "A drink of water, some coffee, something to eat, maybe?"

"No. Go away. Take your hand off me."

"Look," he said, "we don't want you, we don't aim to hurt you. All we want is the fifty thousand dollars your old man's probably already paid for your release. As soon as our partner gets here with the money and we know everything's hunky-dory, we're going to leave here, leave you here. You're going to come out of this okay. Now do you want something—something to eat? You ain't eaten anything since we grabbed you last night. There's some ham and potatoes and gravy downstairs, cold but cooked. One of the girls'll warm you up a meal in no time. How about it, cutie?"

"My name is Dora Shetsher, not Cutie, and I don't want anything to eat, you dirty criminal!"

Gary laughed. "Okay, Dora Shetsher," he said, and turned away.

Buzz snapped off the flashlight. "She'll eat when she gets hungry enough," he said.

Gary said, "Turn the light on. Something wrong here." He had turned back, was leaning low over the girl as he spoke.

Buzz turned the light on.

60

"Hey!" Gary exclaimed. "Come here, Buzz. Well, will you look at that!"

"Look at what?" Buzz went quickly to the bed.

"Look at that!" Gary grabbed up Dora Shetsher's hands, dropped them. He snatched the cords off the bed, held them up for Buzz to see. "The sly little mink untied her hands. Can you beat it? You tied her up. Maybe you was careless."

Buzz grunted. "Careless, hell," he said. "She didn't untie them. Somebody did it for her. Easter—" He stared at Gary, licked his lips. "Yeah. Easter. She was here. Maybe she's still here."

He threw the flash's beam around, went to the wardrobe, tried to open the door. "Get the old man up here." he growled. "I want to see what's behind this door. Call the old lying bastard!"

Gary went out in the hall. "Hey, Danson!" he yelled. "Come up here, Danson!"

Jodie was climbing through Easter's bedroom window when he heard Gary call. He had slipped from the room while Buzz and Gary were looking at the cords he had taken off Dora's wrists. He had been standing behind the door when Buzz and Gary entered the room, and while they were standing by the bed, backs turned to him, talking, examining the loose cords, he had slipped around the door, across the hall, into Easter's bedroom.

Now he crept across the roof of the back porch, over to the corner by the meat house.

"They'll keep a close watch on her from now on," he told himself, climbing down from the roof. "It'll be real tough getting her out of the house now. Real tough."

He was passing in shadow by the meat-house door when he heard a sound like something heavy dropping onto stone. He stopped, moved in close to the door, felt for its knob. His fingers closed on a big steel bolt-and-keeper. The sound had seemed to come from inside the

61

meat house. He put an ear against the door. "Could be a cat or some wild varmint is in there, after the meat," he told himself. He listened a moment longer, then shrugged. "No time to worry about saving somebody else's meat," he told himself, starting to move on. Then he heard another sound, a quite different one—a scraping, raking noise. He stopped, listened. The scraping, raking noise went on, and on.

"Something digging in there," he mused. "A dog maybe got itself closed in there—" He started to move on again, and then he heard a sound like a sob—a hard shuddering sob.

He stopped again, listened. The scraping noises were still going on. Then his heart seemed to plop up into his mouth and his stomach seemed to flop over, as it came to him, "Ruie! Can it be they locked Ruie in there? Can it be—"

He had not heard her voice while he was in the house. He was muttering to himself as he shot back the bolt and yanked the door open, "She got to be too much for them, so they locked her in here! Sure! Sure, it's Ruie! It's Ruie!"

He wanted to shout and laugh, he was that relieved. He did, almost, checking himself, and dodging, just in time to miss having his head split down the middle with the biggest bone cleaver he had ever seen in his life.

Shh-thock! the cleaver smashed into the door jamb only inches away from his head. And there it stood, an inch or more of the corner of its big blade buried in the wood of the sill brace.

He heard it, an instant he saw it, then he was inside the meat house, stooping low, moving cautiously along the darkest wall. Somebody was in here, all right—somebody who had tried to kill him; it was not Ruie, of course. Ruie would not have thrown the bone cleaver at somebody without first knowing who that somebody was. He was certain it was not Ruie. He came to a corner, crouched there in black darkness, watching the door's starlight-paled rectangle.

It was in his mind that whoever was in here wanted out, and in the worst way. He believed if he waited long enough, that person would go out of here, fast and hard. And he believed right, for, suddenly, there was a swishing, thudding sound. Something soft whipped against his leg, and he grabbed out with both hands.

His hands closed on softness. There was a ripping noise. He jerked on what he had in his hands, and it gave. There was another ripping noise, not so loud or so prolonged. Slack came into whatever it was he had in his hands. He felt of it, wadded it, threw it down. A shirt or some kind of garment, he thought.

Someone passed through the door, disappeared. He glimpsed legs, arms, that was all.

He lunged, ran. He was around the meat house and heading for the cow stable when he saw who he was after.

She was running in the open, in bright starlight, leaving the cow stable, heading for the straw stack. She was naked.

He could not be sure in that light, at that distance, but he was almost sure. It was Easter.

"I tore the clothes off her," he told himself, wonderingly. "I stripped her naked there in the dark. Why didn't she say something? Why didn't I say something? What a dumb fool thing to do—strip her naked like that—"

She was almost hidden in the straw, standing and leaning into the side of the stack, when he reached her. She was panting, but smiling. She said, "I saw you when you came by the cow stable. Oh, God help me, but was I glad! I felt like yelling 'Whoopee' when I saw it was you, Jodie!"

He did not look at her, except at her face. "I'm sorry

about ripping your clothes off you like that," he said. "But how was I to know it was you?"

She laughed thinly. "I almost hit you with the bone cleaver. I almost killed you, Jodie."

"You thought I was Buzz or Gary?"

"No." She wagged her head, hard, and stopped laughing. "I thought it was someone else—a big man wearing coveralls and a slouch hat. He was inside our henhouse. He—he chased me. I went into the meat house to get away from him, and he locked me in there. Oh, Jodie, I was sure he would catch me, rape me, kill me, something—Oh, sweet Jesus, I thought for dead sure I was a gone goose."

"A—a man and—and not one of them—not Buzz, not Gary?"

She nodded loosely, went on nodding even after she said, "Yes. A big man, in big, dark floppy coveralls and a dark slouch hat. A big, big man."

"Maybe it was your brother Walt?"

She spent a thoughtful moment staring at him, then shook her head. "He was Walt's size," she mused, but shook her head again. "No. Wasn't Walt. Couldn't have been. Walt wouldn't be caught dead in coveralls. Besides, Walt can't stand the smell of chickens. He stopped going inside the henhouse while he was still in grade school."

"Then who was it?" Jodie asked, and took off his jacket.

Easter shrugged, moved away from the straw. Jodie dropped his jacket on the ground, began unbuttoning his shirt.

"What're doing, Jodie?" Easter asked, frowning in puzzlement.

"You can wear my shirt," he said. "It's got a real long tail. It'll cover more of you than your pajama top did, I guess."

"Jodie, you're not looking at me."

64

"I know." He went on unbuttoning his shirt.

"Don't you like to look at naked girls?"

"Depends on who they are," he said, and took off his shirt, handed it to her.

She took it, but did not put it on. "Am I ugly—to you, am I?"

"No. You're a very pretty girl, Easter."

She dropped his shirt, put her hands under her full breasts, cupped them there, lifted her breasts slightly, pointed them at him, squeezed them, shook them a little. "I've got pretty martens," she said. "Not too big, and not small at all. Do you like them, Jodie?"

"Martens?" he said, and glanced at her breasts, then looked into her eyes. "I never heard them called that before."

"Grandfather Danson always called them that—on a cow, a mare, a woman, on anything they grew on, he called them martens. I don't rightly know where he picked up the word. Maybe he made it up out of his own head. He used to say he made this or that out of his own head, any idea he had or something; then he'd say, 'and after I made it I had enough wood left to build a three-hole privy.' He was a catbird. Uncle Crabtree Danson always said that about him. 'Pap sure is a catbird,' Uncle Crabtree would say when Grandfather had told some wild or dirty joke and everybody, including Grandfather, had bellowed themselves half sick. Sometimes Uncle Crabtree would get really tickled at something Grandfather said, and he'd yip and smack his leg and say, 'Pap sure is a piss-walloper! A real tee-total piss-walloper!' "

"Why don't you put on my shirt?" Jodie asked.

"I'll put it on in a minute. I want you to look at me naked. I want you to see me. Gee, you're stupid in some ways. Don't you know it gives some girls big kicks to have a fellow see them naked? I let Gurley Robinson see me naked once when I was only fifteen.

We were picking blackberries. Nobody else was around close. Just me and pretty little, doll-faced Gurley Robinson there. He had the biggest brownest eyes I ever saw in a human being's face. He had eyes like a Jersey cow, big and brown and soft. We was there in the brambles, picking berries and talking. It was a hot day and there wasn't enough breeze going to blow a chickadee feather off a dry clod. Gurley was talking about how good he could shoot marbles, and all at once I got this idea. I looked at him and said, 'Shut up about marble playing, Gurley, and watch me.'

" 'Don't you tell me to shut up, Easter Danson!' he said, as snappish as a turtle with a crawcrab pinching its butt. 'Don't you tell me—' He shut up then, because I jerked up my dress and unbuttoned my drawers and let them fall and hopped out of them. Then I went skipping round and round poor little Gurley, a-taking off the rest of my clothes and pitching them up in the air and letting them fall all over the blackberry briers. And —and Gurley, he watched me—with them big soft brown eyes. And it was like he was touching my flesh, feeling of me in places where a fellow's feeling of a girl is the best."

She laughed, stepped close to Jodie. She went on laughing, saying, "And I wouldn't let him do it to me. He begged and begged, offered me his berries, offered to pick my bucket the rest of the way full, too, while I sat in the shade. . . . Oh, sweet Jesus, did he beg, and I wouldn't let him do it to me." She shook her head, clucked her tongue. "I was as stupid then as you 'pear to be now," she said.

He picked up his shirt, held it out to her. "I'm not going to give in, Easter," he said, wondering if he really meant it. "I'm not going to make love to you. I wish you'd get that through your thick skull. You're the stupid one, not me."

She laughed again and tossed her head. She was still

66

squeezing her breasts, pointing them at him. Their little dark points would go big, then small, as she squeezed. He thought their little dark point looked like ripe damson plums when they would go big, and when they would go small, they looked like tender, first day rosebuds.

"They're going to kill Dora Shetsher," he said. "Gary told her they would leave her here, unharmed, after Walt got here with the ransom money. But they won't do it. They'll kill her."

She stopped squeezing her breasts, let her hands fall and hang limply at her smooth, firm thighs, and stared at him. "How do you know that?"

"Does it matter how I know it? We've got to do something—I've got to do something. If I only had a gun. I could handle this thing, if I had a gun."

"Did you see Ruie when you went in the house?" she asked, and took his shirt, slowly put it on.

"No. I didn't even hear her voice. I heard the voices of all the others, but not Ruie's. Not even once."

"But you did see the Shetsher girl?"

He nodded. He told her everything that had happened while he was in the house. She had buttoned the shirt all the way down by the time he finished. The tail of it reached to a few inches of her knees. It was sizes and sizes too big for her.

"I guess they changed their minds about fetching Ruie out here, pretending to torture her, having her yell for me?" she said. "I guess Buzz and Aggie changed their minds about that, huh?"

"I don't know," he said.

"You think they hurt her, or something?"

"I thought it was her in the meat house when I heard you. That's why I went in there."

She nodded. "I was digging under the floor with the bone cleaver. I thought I might get out of there before that man came back."

67

"You think he's still around here?"

"I—I guess I don't. He must have been some fellow passing through on foot, decided to steal some chickens; then changed his mind. Or maybe he was after eggs. I guess he must have gone on. He must have locked me in the meat house so I couldn't cause a ruckus and get folks out chasing him."

Jodie nodded. "He probably moved on," he said, looking all around, at the cow stable, the henhouse, the meat house, the house. "Dora Shetsher's nothing like you said," he told her. "She's not one bit puny, and she's pretty. She's not a kid, either. She's twenty if she's a day."

She nodded. "I know. She didn't have anything on 'cept a bathing suit, a Bikini, nothing but a couple of strings, when they got her out of the car. Ruie gave her an old kimona of mine. She's a sweet looker, all right. I wanted you to feel good'n sorry for her; that's why I lied about her age and all."

He stared at her, and was silent. She was everything wrong she could be, lewd, dishonest, perhaps evil. He had never known anyone like her before, and he was afraid of her—in a strange way he was—a way he did not understand. It was something like the fear he had had when he had been near someone who had a catching disease, and he had thought about it afterwards, pictured himself coming down with it.

It was more like that than anything else he could think of—like being afraid of catching the smallpox or scarlet fever. And there was something else, another bad feeling that he had about her, a feeling that she wanted something from him, something he could not give her without ruining himself, spoiling his life, his future. Worse than anything else, though, was the way he was beginning to want her, want to make love to her.

"I wonder what time it is?" Easter said.

He looked at his wrist watch. He had some difficulty in reading the position of the hands, but finally did. "Quarter of one."

He picked up his jacket, was putting it on when she said, "Do you always go without an undershirt, like now?"

"Only in the summer."

"Gee, you're nicely built. You got a very handsome chest, and very manly arms and shoulders. You're strong, all right. I found that out when you choked me a while ago."

"I'm sorry about that," he said. "I got a mean temper. It's not good for me when I lose it."

She laughed thinly. "It's not good for the other fellow, either."

He glanced out at the house. "I got to go back in there," he said. "I got to get Dora Shetsher and Ruie out of there."

She nodded. "I know. I got a plan for getting them out. I think it'll work, too."

"Yes? I'd like to hear it."

She sat down on the straw that Buzz had kicked up with his feet while he was making love to Aggie. She leaned back against the stack. "Sit down here beside me, Jodie," she said, and patted the straw.

"Are you going to try it again, Easter?" He glared down at her, not moving.

She laughed softly. "No. Sit down. I'll tell you about my plan for you getting the girls out of the house."

He sat down. She stared at him for a moment, then said. "I'll scream and scream. That's my plan."

He looked at her, puzzled, said, "Oh?"

She nodded. "They'll hear me in the house. They'll come tearing out here. While they're out here, running around like chickens with their heads chopped off, you run into the house, let Dora Shetsher loose. Then you, her and Ruie skin outside, hide around somewhere.

Maybe in the fields across the road from the barn. There's a lot of big bushes over there."

He stared at her for a long moment. "It just might work. When do you want to try to pull it off?"

"In a few minutes," she said, smiling at him. "As soon as you—you make love to me. In a—a few minutes. It won't take long for you to make love to me, not the way I feel . . . not the way I can make you feel. . . ."

He only stared at her. After a few seconds, he got up and started to walk away.

"Wait, Jodie!" she said. "Don't be sore at me, Jodie. Please. Wait."

He heard her get up and come after him. He did not look back. He kept on walking, heading for the cow stable. It was just as she caught up to him and took hold of his arm that they heard a door slam.

They stopped, looking over toward the house. They saw a man and a girl hurrying away from the kitchen door, across the back yard. The man was holding the girl by the arm.

"That's Ruie!" Jodie said, and they both turned around. They went back to the straw stack, bent over and running.

They were on top of the straw stack again, lying on their bellies, heads up, peeking through the straw, by the time Gary and Ruie reached the cow stable. "Now you're going to get a good look at Gary Summerfield," Easter said, glancing at Jodie and frowning. "I mean you are, if you can take your eyes off of Ruie long enough."

She shook her head and made a wondering face. "I guess I was never in love," she mused, lowering her voice. "Gary's not anything that a girl might want to hang on her Christmas tree," she went on, after a moment spent in watching Gary and Ruie climb over the stable lot fence. "But he's big and husky and not bad

70

to look at; only thing is, he's a glutton—got the appetite of a full-grown boar hog in March, craves to eat up everything in sight—food, liquor, girls ... He likes to fight, too. I went to school with him, don't forget. I know what a lowdown, no-good dog he is."

"Was he always Walt's friend?"

"Always, for as far back as I can remember. They're pups of the same litter. Wasn't anybody around here would have much to do with either of them, so they strung along together. Grew up that way, stringing along together, fighting, stealing, ruffling the girls that'd let them, and some that wouldn't let them. Got drunk together once on jug-dreenings when Walt was ten and Gary was eight. Started hellin' around before they were dry behind the ears. Gary's about twenty-three now, and look what he's mixed up in. Kidnapping. My God!"

"His folks still live around here?"

"Yes, Seven farms down the road. And they ain't much. His old man makes moonshine whiskey, sells what he and his old lady don't drink up. And he doesn't sell very much, either."

Jodie nodded, staring at Ruie. He could not look at Gary for looking at her. She was not hurt or sick or changed in any way that he could see; and thank God for that! She was wearing short-shorts and a man's work shirt that was sizes too big for her. He guessed she wore a halter under the shirt, and had put the shirt on when the kidnappers arrived. He knew she never wore short-shorts and halter when there was a chance strangers would see her. She was not like most girls he knew; she had a very deep modest streak in her; and he liked that; he liked girls to be modest and ladylike.

"You think you can lick him?" Easter asked.

He nodded, still watching Ruie. "I can lick him," he said.

"He's got a gun, and he knows how to use it."

"I can still lick him." He glanced at Gary, and it was

71

all right. He did not have any more doubts; he was not thinking like a punk kid any more. Gary was holding Ruie's arm plenty tight; he would give him an extra wallop in the face for that. He would give the big monkey a couple of extra wallops just for putting his hands on her.

"I didn't think he'd go along with Buzz's plan," Easter said. "I wonder why he is going along with it? He knows I won't come running and be grabbed, not even if Ruie would squall her head off. He must have something else in mind. He must just want to get her out here alone. He always did have a case on her, but she was too high and mighty to have anything to do with him. Now maybe he's going to make her pay for her high-and-mightiness."

"You hate Ruie," Jodie said, not looking at her.

"Maybe I do," she replied. "Maybe that's why I want you to make love to me so much—because I hate her."

"She's good and decent and honest and very intelligent, and pretty, too, and you hate her for all those things—because she's better and smarter than you."

"She's not prettier than I am."

"Maybe she's not, but she's pretty enough. Not many girls can match her for looks."

"Aw, you're just gone on her. You're just a high-school kid suffering from puppy love. You don't know anything about a real honest-to-goodness girl. If you'd get really acquainted with me, you'd never have anything more to do with Ruie. You'd drop her like as if she was a cold dead toad that somebody put in your hand when you wasn't looking."

"You're rotten," Jodie said, not looking at her, looking only at Ruie.

"You're a dumb nut fool."

When Gary and Ruie were near enough to the straw stack for what they said to be heard, they stopped talking. Easter wriggled around until her thigh was hard against Jodie's; then she lay very still, as they heard Gary say, "It was Buzz's idea, not mine. He thinks Easter'll give herself up if we can convince her we're going to really hurt you if she don't. So all you have to do is yell, cry, carry on, act like I'm beating you. I'll only smack you easy-like. I won't hurt you at all."

"Why didn't you back me up in there?" Ruie asked, angrily. "Why didn't you tell them I was telling the truth when I said Easter wouldn't show herself if you beat me to death? You know Easter—you know she's always hated me—she'd be glad if you beat me!"

"It was Buzz's idea—I told you that once." Gary said. "I didn't want to tell him it wouldn't work. He thinks it's rich stuff. I didn't want to make him feel bad. It puffs him up when somebody pays attention to his ideas. I like Buzz."

"You lie." Ruie glared up at him as they passed into the shadow of the straw stack. "You only wanted to get me out here alone. Why? What have you got on your scrubby little mind, Gary Summerfield?"

They stopped. Gary let go of her arm. "Don't try to run or anything," he said. "You'll just be wasting your energy if you do. You know you can't outrun me."

"I'm not going to try to outrun you," Ruie said. "Why did you bring me out here? What do you want? Or maybe I should ask, what do you think you can get?"

"I got a notion that Walt's double-crossed us," Gary said. "If he has, we're in kind of a bad spot. No money. That girl on our hands. The law looking for us. Buzz and I told Walt if he didn't show up here in a reasonable time, we'd kill his old man and anybody else that was here. I don't think I meant it, but Buzz meant it. He's killed before. I never have. I never want to. But Buzz meant it, and if Walt doesn't show by daylight I got a notion he'll do what he said—kill your father, Dora Shetsher, you, and Easter if he can find her."

"And you'd let him?" Ruie said, her voice thick with

disgust. "You'd let him kill that girl, kill us? You used to be our neighbor. Your folks are still our neighbors. Doesn't that mean anything to you? I've known you since I can remember. You and Easter and Walt and I went to school and church together. Gary, you must be crazy—"

"Dora Shetsher can identify us if we're ever caught," he said. "She can bring the law to this farm. We've got to kill her to save our own skins. You know that. If I thought it could be any other way for her, then I would be what you said—crazy."

"Do you realize what you're saying, Gary?" Ruie asked in a low, outraged tone. "Do you, really?"

Gary shrugged. "Sure." He was staring at her. He shrugged again. "I'm in this with the others. We agreed to take a vote on anything important that came up. We took a vote on the Shetsher girl awhile ago. It was three to one in favor of killing her. So I got to go along with the vote."

"And kill me, and Papa, if that's how the vote on us goes?"

He nodded. "I got to go along with the others." He reached to take hold of her arm, but she stepped back and said, "I'm not going to let on like I'm being hurt when it isn't so. If there was a chance I could help you catch Easter by pretending you were beating me, I wouldn't do it. She's my sister. She hates me. But I don't hate her. I don't want her caught. Maybe she's all wrong in her mind—she is crazy in a way, I guess—but I don't want you and Buzz to get your hands on her. I'll do anything I can to prevent it, too."

"Oh, you would, huh?" Gary grabbed for her arm again, and got it, squeezed it until she winced. "Well, I want her caught," he said. "She was in the house a while ago and tried to turn Dora Shetsher loose. She'd have done it, too, if Buzz and I hadn't happened to

74

come upstairs when we did. So I want her caught. I got the feeling she's going to be the cause of us all going to jail. I got the feeling real strong."

"Go catch her, then," Ruie said. "For I'm not going to yell unless I have something to yell about."

"I can sure give you something to yell about," Gary said, his voice all at once going solid, his words hitting hard. "I don't reckon Walt would kick up too much of a fuss if I roughed you up a little." He gave her a thin-lipped grin. "You ever get punched in the face right hard, Ruie?" he asked, and held his fist up in front of her nose.

"No," she said, glaring at him.

He chopped out a short laugh. "I might even rape you," he said. "I reckon you'd yell if I started ripping that shirt and that other litty-bitty stuff off you—"

"You can't scare me, Gary. There's no need for you to try."

"I'm not trying to scare you. I'm trying to decide whether to black your eyes and bloody your nose, or rip your clothes off and throw you down here in the straw." He gave her the thin-lipped grin again. "You think I'm kidding ... you really do think I'm kidding."

He jerked her up against him, hard, put his arms around her, looked down into her face. He laughed. "Something tells me I start in to rape you, I'm not going to stop till I get it done, no matter how much you yell," he said. Then, his grin softening somewhat, he put his face very close to hers. He said, "I always did crave to have you, baby. Way back when we were just kids I often thought about it, and wanted to do it. Now I got my chance.'"

"You brought me out here for this, and that's all," Ruie said, and tried to wriggle free. He held her and laughed, and in a moment or so she stopped trying to get away.

75

6

JODIE said, "You stay here. If I flub this, you go phone the sheriff. I don't care if you have to walk five miles, you go. You heard what Gary said. They're going to kill Dora Shetsher. You can bet they'll kill your father and Ruie, too, if I can't stop them."

She stared into his eyes, then nodded. He nodded back.

"Walt's not coming," she said. "He double-crossed them."

"That's what they've decided."

"Gary said—said Buzz had killed before."

He nodded again.

She sighed, glanced out at the house. "Don't flub, it, Jodie."

He turned on his buttocks and crawled away from her, away from the side of the stack that shadowed Gary and Ruie. When he reached the stack's edge, he paused, looked back at Easter. She was watching him intently.

He heard Gary give a harsh laugh. He went down the stack, headfirst, holding onto the straw to keep from going down too fast. He was flattening his hands on the ground when he glimpsed the shadow of a man move and join his shadow on the earth. He twisted away from a sound of rustling, and was falling when consciousness quit him, quit him completely.

Consciousness came back slowly, fuzzily, painfully. He was trying to get up off his face when he first knew that he was who he was, and that he was trying to do anything at all. For a frantic, motionless moment, he thought he had somehow swallowed his tongue. Then, trying to make sure about it, he thought, more frantically, that his mouth was mashed in and all his teeth were gone.

He wanted to say, "Oh, God!" He tried to say it, and could not. Then, with hot, surging relief, it came to him that he was gagged, that a thick, dry rag was tied in his mouth. In the next instant, he knew he was tied, helplessly tied, hand and foot. He gasped, managed to turn off his belly onto his back.

A thumping pain at the back of his head told him he had been slugged. "But how long ago?" he asked himself. "But, oh, God, how long ago?" He tried his bonds, mightily, first those at his wrists, then those at his ankles. He strained until pain shot through and through his shoulders, his groin. "Ruie—what happened? Did Gary —God help me! Did Gary—did he—did he—did he—?"

And what had happened to Easter to keep her from knowing he was slugged, to keep her from coming down here, after his attacker left, and freeing him? Had they got Easter?

They had. Of course they had.

And they would get him—just give them time. But it was not Gary who had slugged him. It was not Buzz. Buzz had been in the house, guarding Dora Shetsher. Surely, it was not Aggie or Emma. Then—the big man in the dark coveralls and slouch hat—the big man who had chased Easter and locked her in the meat house— Yeah, the big man—

He cursed, began to chew at the gag. He stabbed his heels into the earth and shoved with his legs, shoved himself in, then began shoving himself around the stack. Suddenly he stopped all movement, held his breath, listened. He had heard a sound, a sound like a voice . . .

There! There it was again! "Please, Gary," it said. "Don't do this to me! I—I've always tried so hard to be a good person. Gary, I'd rather be dead than—than

77

treated like this, humiliated like this. Please, Gary! Beat me. I'll scream if you beat me enough. But please don't do this to me!"

"Ruie!" Jodie frothed against the gag. "Ruie—" He tried to relax a little, tried not to pant so, telling himself that he still had time. If he could only get loose, somehow, he still had time. If Easter would only come to him—Where was she? What had happened to her? If she was still on the stack, she could see him, even now, if she would stretch her neck a little and look down this way. Where was she?

An instant later, he knew how he could free himself of his bonds. But it was so far away—the means of freedom was so very far away—he might be seen going there, shoving himself over the grass with his heels, riding his shoulderblades across the cow lot, past the cow stable. . . . He probably would be seen. He had to go around the stack past it, and the grass was not high enough to conceal him entirely. Gary would probably see him, unless, God forbid, he was too busy doing to Ruie what he had threatened. And how long would it take? Five minutes—ten? Too long, too long . . . Would Gary hold off that long? Would Ruie's attempts to reason and plead with him hold him off that long?

"Anyway, it's the only thing I can do," he told himself. "The only thing—the only chance—"

He rolled over and around, onto his back. He pointed himself toward the house, drew up his legs, stabbed his heels into the sod, quickly straightened his legs. He moved about two feet, maybe a little more. Two feet, he thought. Two feet with every hitch. He must travel no less than four hundred feet. "Two hundred hitches," he said to himself, squirming his tongue against the gag. "Two hundred hitches, less the one I just made."

He drew up his legs and stabbed his heels into the sod. He could do it. He had to do it.

Easter lay flat out on her belly in the straw, hands spread on cheeks, elbows resting on Jodie's jacket, and watched—watched Gary and Ruie, watched Jodie; and it was difficult for her to know which entertained her the most. Ruie was going to get her comeuppance soon; and that would be something to see and hear. Gary was not going to mess around with her much longer. He had already stripped her. He was trying to get her to make love, do her part as though she enjoyed it. But he would not just go on and on coaxing forever. Easter knew. She could tell by his voice, the way it was getting thicker and thicker, hoarser and hoarser; also she could tell by the things he said, wanted Ruie to say. He was teasing Ruie to work up his courage, she knew. She had been raped three times, and one of those times by Gary. She knew how Gary operated; she knew that just when Ruie thought she had talked him out of it, that's when it would happen.

But getting raped was a lot different with her than it was with Ruie. She had wanted to be raped, and had only put up a fight to make it more interesting, to see exactly what the fellow would do. She had always been careful to give in before he really hurt her.

But Ruie was truly frightened by what Gary was doing, and Ruie had told the truth when she had told Gary she would rather be dead than raped. Easter, watching Jodie hitch his way on his shoulders through the near knee-high grass toward the cow stable, listened and grinned as Ruie begged. Then, all at once, she was not listening to Ruie, and she was not watching Jodie. She was staring out toward the road, staring at a man walking there, coming through the field from the road, walking toward her—a big man wearing dark, floppy coveralls and a dark slouch hat.

"He slugged Jodie and tied him up," she told herself, licking her lips and staring, "and then he left, and I thought he left for good. But he came back. Oh, my God!"

She had never been so afraid of anyone in her life as she was of the man in the floppy coveralls. It was not like her to be much afraid of any man, and she could not understand the way she felt, the tightness under her breasts, the dryness in her throat, and her heart racing so . . . The man had chased her, locked her in the meat house, but he had not tried to harm her. He had slugged Jodie and tied him up, and she wondered why he had done it. But neither of these things was responsible for the awful way she felt about him. It was something else, something she did not know about, something she only felt. It was like when sometimes she would meet a strange dog when she was alone, would take one look at it and right away know if it was going to wag its tail or try to bite her. It was like that, this fear of the man in the floppy coveralls—it was intuition, that's what it was. And it was awful.

"It's like I know he's going to catch me and kill me, and how can that be? How can I know a thing like that?"

He was coming out from the cow stable now, hurrying. She glanced to her left, at Jodie, saw him flat on his back in the grass. He had seen or heard the man; the way he was lying, so still, told her so. But the man had not seen him; the man was already past him, was still hurrying straight toward the straw stack.

Suddenly Ruie screamed.

Easter almost screamed, herself, she was so startled. She went stiff to her toes, gave a little gasp. She softly whispered to herself, "Poor Jodie . . . what he must be suffering now . . ." The man started to run, still heading toward the stack. Ruie screamed again, and he ran faster. And Easter said to herself, "Serves her right. Jodie, too."

Easter looked around, down at Gary and Ruie. Gary

80

was on top of Ruie, was choking her, was telling her to spread her legs or he would kill her. Ruie was on her back, her legs twisted around each other. She was clawing, hitting at Gary's face, trying to bite his arms. He went on choking her. He was still choking her when the man in the floppy coveralls came round the stack, stepped in close and kicked him hard in the back of the head...

Jodie's shoulders were numb, no feeling at all left in them; but he knew how they were—skin raked off, bleeding. He was panting and drenched with perspiration. But that did not matter, his hurt shoulders did not matter. Only Ruie mattered—Ruie who might be dead, who might have been raped by now... He did not want to think about that. He had heard her scream twice, then had seen the man in the floppy coveralls disappear behind the straw stack. After that he had not heard anything. So the man had stopped Gary—anyway, he believed that was what had happened—the man had stopped Gary. And what had he done to Ruie?

With these thoughts pounding through his mind, Jodie lay on his back and stared up through the gloom at his means of freedom. He had made it to the right place, and now all he had to do—

He wriggled forward slightly, lifted his legs, and put his feet against the jamb of the meat-house door. The big bone cleaver was just above him, the fore corner of its big blade buried in the door jamb, a goodly length of its chopping edge in plain view. He stared at it, wriggled his shoulders, his buttocks, and inch by inch his bound-together feet moved up the door jamb, moved up it until he was practically standing on his shoulders, and the cords that bound his ankles were against the blade. A quick, small surge of himself, then, and the cords parted on the sharp steel, fell away. He was up

81

on his feet in a moment. In another moment his wrist cords were against the blade, were cut across and falling away.

He ran around the meat house, on toward the cow stable and the straw stack, rubbing his wrists. He cleared the rear corner of the cow stable, paused, looked all around, saw no one. An impulse, difficult to control, was driving him to yell Ruie's name at the top of his lungs. He did not pause again, not until he came around the straw stack and saw what was there. Then he stopped all over at once—stopped like he had run up against a stone wall.

The two bodies lay straight away from each other on their bellies, their feet touching. They lay still—too still. Ruie was naked.

Shock held him motionless for a moment, then he was on his knees beside Ruie, turning her, lifting her, holding her close, with her high breasts soft against his chest. And he felt her heart, beating against his own. Their chests were pressed so tightly together that he thought it was his heart at first—then he knew different. It was her heart. She was alive.

"Ruie!" he said, whispering hoarsely. "Ruie, it's Jodie! Ruie . . ."

She stirred and opened her eyes. For a moment there was nothing in them except the starlight; then she was in them, the love was in them, warmly, brightly. "Jodie! Oh, darling!"

The stone was as big as his head. It whapped the earth beside him. He whirled around, bending far over to shield Ruie—saw another one coming, and tried to dodge it. He did not know when it hit him.

He came to, crawling; for a fuzzy, pain-filled moment he went on crawling. Then he remembered. He stopped, tried to get onto his feet and fell on his face. He tried again, and made it to his knees.

He blinked, peering about. He was on the wrong side

of the straw stack. He wondered, "My God, how long have I been crawling around!" He tried to get onto his feet again, made it, and went lurching around the straw stack. He saw Gary, but not Ruie. He tripped and fell over Gary before he could get stopped. Ruie was not here.

He went on, crawling again, and saw Easter. He tried to yell at her. She was running toward the cow stable. She had a gun in her hand.

His attempt to yell brought a small croaking sound, it felt like, from his belly. He tried again—the same croaking sound. He started to go after Easter, looking around as he ran, lurching. A few steps more and he fell, fell into a crazy, impossible hole of solid blackness that had suddenly opened in the starlight in front of him.

This time he came to with somebody saying, "Jodie! Jodie, wake up! Please, Jodie!"

He opened his eyes. He was looking up into Easter's face. Easter was sitting on the ground, holding his head in her bare lap. He stared at her, blinked, and stared some more, wanting to scream and scream because she was not Ruie—wanting to beat her, strangle her, because she was not Ruie.

"Jodie," Easter said, "Walt's here. Do you hear—do you understand, Jodie? Walt's here. The big man in the floppy coveralls. I got a good look at his face when he hit you in the head with the rock. He's Walt. He's Walt, Jodie; and I think he killed Gary. He kicked and kicked and kicked him in the head, and I think he killed him."

"Wh-what did he do to Ruie?"

"Nothing. He swore awful when he saw who she was. She fainted before he kicked Gary in the head. She screamed twice, and Gary was about to rape her; then she fainted. Walt just looked at her and swore, then he went away, went over toward the house, went behind it. The next time I saw him he was following you out to the straw stack from the cow stable. He came up behind you while you was holding Ruie in your arms, and threw a rock at you. He missed. He threw another— you know what happened then."

"Wh-where were you wh-when all that was happening?"

"On top of the straw stack where you left me— where you told me to stay."

"Why didn't you come down and untie me? You saw Walt slug me—" He felt of his head, groaned. "Why didn't you help me?"

"Yes, I saw it. But I didn't know it was Walt then, and I was afraid. Jodie, I was never so afraid in my whole life. I couldn't move. Honest! I wanted to help you, but I couldn't move."

He stared into her face, and did not believe her. He noticed she was wearing his jacket, and recalled she had not been wearing it when he had seen her running away from the straw stack with the gun in her hand. "You—you went and got Gary's gun," he said. "Then you ran away. You knew I was there, dazed and crawling around. But you ran away."

"Ruie was dazed, too," she said. "I was trying to catch her. She was staggering around, running and staggering. I tried to catch her, but she was too near the house when I first noticed her. She went into the house before I could reach her."

"Ruie went back in the house?" he said, and was shaken by what seemed a tidal wave of frustration. "You—you let her go back in the house?"

"I couldn't stop her. I tried."

"You lie!" he husked. "You lie! It's like I can smell lies all over you—it's like your lies are old rotten manure, and I can smell the stink of them all over you. Ruie didn't go in the house. You did something to her. You took her away from the straw stack. You tied her up and hid her somewhere. By God, you did—you did something to her—"

84

"I didn't do anything to her," Easter told him calmly. "I told the truth. Honest to God, Jodie, I told the truth! About everything—I did!"

"You dirty liar!" he said, looking around. She said nothing. A moment later, he asked, "Where are we? I've never been here before."

"Behind the henhouse," Easter said. "The wall there is the back wall of the henhouse. The door is around the corner to your left. These vines are grapevines. We used to have a grape arbor here. It's a better place to hide than at the straw stack."

"How did I get here?"

"Walked and crawled. I helped you most of the way. You were dazed. You were mumbling. You almost passed out, a couple of times."

He felt of his head, and had no difficulty finding the hurts. "Gary didn't—didn't rape Ruie, did he?" he asked.

"No. He was about to. But she wouldn't uncross her legs. He was choking her. She fainted and he could have, but Walt kicked him in the head before he could let go of her throat."

"And—and Ruie went in the house? Honest Injun?"

She nodded. "Yes." She moved slightly, and his jacket and shirt gaped open. Her round breasts plumped into view and she made a little cross between them with her finger. She said, "Cross my heart and hope to die."

She was lying—he knew it. He tried to believe her, and could not. "Have you still got Gary's gun?" he asked.

"Gary's gun?" she mused, staring into his eyes and shaking her head. "Did I ever have it?"

"I saw a gun in your hand when you ran away from the straw stack," he told her. "If it wasn't Gary's, whose was it?"

She looked at him curiously, smiled. "You imagined it was a gun," she replied. "It was only a stick I picked up—picked up for no reason at all."

85

He started to tell her he had seen it clearly, and that it was a gun; then he changed his mind. She was lying about having the gun; she probably had it on her, in his jacket pocket, right now. He sat up, smoothed back his hair with his palms. He knew Easter was looking at his back. "How does it look, pretty bad?"

"The skin's rubbed off in spots, over your shoulder-blades," she said. "You're all smeared with grass stain. How'd you ever manage to get yourself untied, Jodie?"

He told her how. "It wasn't easy, going all that way on my heels and shoulders, but—well, I was a high-school fullback, remember."

"I called you some wrong names," she said. "Coward. Sissy. I'm sorry. I didn't really mean anything by them, though. I was just sore because you wouldn't make love to me."

She paused, looked at him, solemnly. They were sitting on the ground, on thick grass. Her thigh was lightly touching his hip. Her long, pretty legs were straight away in front of her, and spread a little. She was quiet for a long moment. He glanced at her. She smiled and said, "Jodie, Walt collected the ransom money—fifty thousand dollars. And it's here somewhere. What if we'd happen to find it, you or me? What if we would, Jodie?"

"Well, we'd just find it, that's all. But you're just making talk. You don't know for sure that Walt collected the ransom. You're only guessing."

"Guessing?" She was watching him appraisingly, and he did not like it. She was looking at him the way she might consider a dressed chicken before she started cutting it up. "I'm not guessing, Jodie," she said finally. "If he'd failed to collect the ransom, he would have gone straight into the house as soon as he arrived here and told his friends about it. He wouldn't be acting like he has, sneaking around, jumping onto you and Gary,

86

chasing me. He got the ransom money, okay. And you know what?"

He waited for her to go on.

"I think he came back here to kill Gary and Buzz and Dora Shetsher. I think he figures it's the only way he can ever feel safe—killing them, having them dead. He said something to Gary after he kicked him unconscious. He swore, and he said, 'Why'd you bring those tramps here? Why'd you and Buzz have to let them in on our game? Goddamn you, I hope I killed you.' That's what he said. So, you see, he didn't already know Aggie and Emma were here."

"Well, so what does that prove?"

"I don't know," she replied. "Maybe nothing. Only I got the idea while he was cussing Gary when Gary couldn't hear him, that he was sore because he had found he was going to have to kill five people instead of three. I guess the way I figured doesn't make much sense. But it's the way I felt when he was cussing Gary."

"Where did Walt go?" Jodie asked. "Where was he when you saw him last?"

"Over by the barn, searching the cars Gary and Buzz drove out here."

Jodie stood up, looked all around. "He might be anywhere now," he said. "He might be hiding here in the brush, watching us, hearing everything we say. I don't think much of your choice of a hiding place. Anybody could sneak up on us here, grab us or throw down on us with a gun before we knew they were around. I like the straw stack better."

"But Walt will come over here sooner or later," she protested. "He hid something in the henhouse, maybe the ransom money. Whatever it is, he'll come back for it, give him time. I feel certain he will."

"If you think he hid something in the henhouse, let's go in there and search."

She shook her head. "I already did. I made a good search."

"Without a light?"

"Y-yes."

"Some search, feeling around in the dark," he said. "Did you go through all Gary's pockets when you took his gun?"

"Yes—no, I didn't—"

He reached over and slapped his jacket pockets—did it so quickly that she could not prevent it. The gun was there, in the inside pocket. He felt some cartridges in a side pocket. He reached into the other side pocket and pulled out a wallet. "Liar," he said, and threw the wallet in her lap. "You even stole his money."

She put the wallet back where he had found it. "I've got a right to lie," she said, and stared into his eyes. "I'm all alone in this thing, so far. You won't help me. I daren't ask any of the others to help me. I'm trying to get my hands on fifty thousand dollars—think of it, fifty thousand dollars! And I'm sure to God trying against plenty heavy odds. If—if you'd help me a—a lot of things would be easier, and—and Dora Shetsher and Ruie might make out a lot better, too. . . ."

"What do you mean by that?" he demanded.

"Well, I—I lied, I lied to you plenty. Ruie and Dora aren't in the house. Ruie went in the house like I said, but she came back out of it in a few minutes, and Dora was with her. I know where they are. And they're not going to get away from where they are—they're going to be dead before daylight, unless—unless you'll come over on my side—help me, really help me."

He stared at her and they were silent for a moment. Then he sighed loudly and said, "You're just plain nuts. You lie all the time. How can I help you when I don't trust you? You don't seem to have any scruples at all, not even one. And you hate Ruie. I guess you hate everybody, maybe even yourself."

88

"You just don't know me, Jodie," she said. "I don't hate you. I think I've fallen in love with you."

He gave a low, mirthless laugh. "You don't know the meaning of love, you don't even know the meaning of honesty. You don't know anything about Dora and Ruie, either."

"I know a heap more about love than you do," she said, nodding at him and smiling. "I know that you're in love with me, and that's something about love that you don't know—yet. I—I—Jodie, I'll share the fifty thousand with you if you'll just let yourself act toward me the way you really want to act toward me . . . We'll go far away, to the coast, maybe. We'll have plenty of money. We'll have each other. We'll be very very happy, Jodie."

He started to speak, then stopped. He was peering through the brush, out toward the straw stack, and just as he started to tell her how crazy she was, how much he disliked her, he saw Gary Summerfield stagger out from the shadow of the straw stack, stop, stand and weave, then move on, staggering, toward the house.

"You were wrong about Walt killing Gary," he said. "There goes Gary now, going to the house. And if what you said is true—if Dora Shetsher isn't in the house— Gary's going to come back out of it mighty quick, and Buzz will be with him. Emma and Aggie, too."

Easter got up onto her feet and watched Gary. "If they all leave the house except my father, then Walt will go in. For he won't want Papa around when he kills the others. He'll want Papa off by himself somewhere, where he'll be safe."

He looked at her wonderingly. "You really think Walt means to kill Dora and his friends, don't you?" he said.

She nodded. "He's not thinking of killing Papa and Ruie, but he's thinking of killing everybody else around here, including me. He hates me as much as I hate him, and I'll sure kill him if I get the chance."

He looked at her and shook his head slightly. "It sure to God stumps me," he said, "how Ruie can be such a good sweet intelligent girl and have folks like she has, a sister like you, a brother like Walt. It sure to God plumb stumps me."

7

JASON DANSON nervously combed his scraggly gray whiskers with scrawny, work-scarred fingers, and squinted across the chimney of the oil lamp at his older daughter.

"Ruie," he said, and his reedy voice quavered oddly, "I want you and this poor girl to go to the Fenser farm, and hurry. When you get there, you tell Casey Fenser all about what's going on here, and ask him to drive you into town. Casey'll do it. He'll be glad to do it. Don't worry about that. When you get to town, you go to the sheriff's house and you tell the sheriff what's going on here. And don't leave out nothing. You put me and Walt in this mess right where we belong. You hear me now, Ruie?"

Ruie nodded. She had been in the house only long enough to put on one of Easter's work dresses and comb her hair, and tell her father what had happened out by the straw stack. Then Gary had come staggering into the house and said that Walt was here, had attacked him, kicked him almost to death.

"I got a good look at him," Gary had mumbled, "right after he kicked me the first time. It was Walt. He was dressed like I never saw him dressed before. Had on coveralls and a slouch hat, and the hat pulled low over his face. But it was Walt, all right. And—and we got to go out there and find him. We—we don't, he'll finish off the lot of us."

At first Buzz had not believed Gary. He had said, "if Walt's out there, why don't he come on in here? What reason would he have for not coming on in here? What you just said don't make good sense, Gary."

"Oh, it makes good sense, all right," Gary had answered. "He's got the ransom money, that's why he doesn't come on in here—why he didn't come on in here first thing. And now he's aiming to kill the lot of us so's he can keep all the money for himself. I reckon he thought he did kill me. He damn nigh kicked my head plumb off of my shoulders. Just looky here—look at that big bruise there over my ear, and that bigger one higher up."

Buzz, Aggie and Emma had looked at the bruises, hastily. Then Buzz had said, "We got to go out there and find that no-good bastard. All of us, 'cept the old man. He stays here and guards the girl, and you—" He had jerked his head around and stared at Ruie. "You stay here with your old man. You leave this house before we get back and I'll—by God, I'll kill you!"

They had gone outside then, Buzz in the lead, and Gary, unsteadily, fetching up the rear. And when they were gone, Jason Danson had gone upstairs and untied Dora Shetsher, come back downstairs with her beside him. Ruie had met him at the bttom of the stairs. He had told her, then, what he wanted her to do.

"You'll be arrested and put in jail," Ruie said. "You know that, don't you, Papa?"

"I know it," Jason replied. "And I'm not expecting anything else to happen to me, 'cept that. Gary fixing to rape you—that tied the dog in the chickenhouse as far as I was concerned. By God, I'll stand for a lot—even having this girl brought here, when Walt wanted to do it so bad. But I'll be everlastingly damned to sucking

91

rotten eggs for the rest of my life, if I'm going to stand by and do nothing when a goddamned, low-lifed, yaller-gutted Summerfield tries to do horny-ka-boogery to my daughter. So you git, Ruie. Go do what I said—go fast and go careful, and do what I said."

Ruie gazed at him for a moment, then stood on tip-toes and kissed him through his whiskers. "I'll do it, Papa," she assured him, wiping tears off her cheeks with her palms. "I'll go do it, just like you said, Papa."

They left the house by the front way, with Jason opening the door for them, and stepping out on the porch to make sure no one was around on that side of the house. They went down the lane, close together, holding hands, and out past the barn, into the road. Then, when they had traveled about two hundred feet down the road, a cow bawled in the field near the road fence. Dora Shetsher gave a startled gasp, and stopped dead in her tracks. Ruie laughed softly and squeezed her hand. "It's just a cow," she said. "My, you must be a city girl. Didn't you ever hear a cow bawl before?"

Dora Shetsher did not say anything for a moment. She seemed to be looking at the cow, which had low-ered its head and was grazing. Ruie squeezed, tugged her hand slightly. "It isn't the cow," Dora said, not mov-ing. "I've seen many cows. I'm not afraid of them. It's that—that girl over there in the shadow of that post, pointing the gun at us. I stopped because of her. Wh-who do you suppose she is? Should we run or stand still?"

Ruie saw the girl with the gun before Dora finished speaking. "She's my sister," she said, flatly. "Don't run. She's just goofy enough to take a shot at you if you do."

Easter gave a short, brittle laugh. She was squatting beside the fence post, and remained squatting as she said, "I guess Papa lost his nerve. I figured something like this might happen when I saw the others run out

92

of the house. Where were you and little sweetie pie headed, Ruie—to the Fenser place?"

"Yes," Ruie replied.

"Figures. Casey Fenser's the only man hereabouts Papa'd trust in a case like this. Well, you're not going to the Fenser place tonight, dearie—you're not going anywhere tonight, and neither is your friend, little sweetie-pie."

She stood up, walked slowly toward them, keeping the gun trained on Ruie, smiling. "I bet you're just dying to know if Jodie's okay. I bet you'd give anything you own to know where he is, if he's alive or dead. Well, I know where he is. I know if he's alive or dead. I could take you to him right now if I wanted. But I don't want. So you're just going to have to be curious and suffer, decent sister. And you're going to have to do what I tell you—you and sweet little rich girl, too—everything I tell you."

Ruie drew a deep breath, let it out slowly, glaring at Easter. She said to Dora, "She's as bad as Walt, maybe worse—she wants to be away from here, be her own boss, so bad it's driving her crazy. We'll have to do what she wants. She'll hurt us if we don't. She might even kill us."

Dora nodded. "Do you want to hold me for ransom, too?" she asked Easter.

Easter grinned. "I might. But that's not the idea at the moment. Right now I don't want the sheriff to get hold of you. He does, this farm will be overrun with deputies in less than an hour. And I don't want any deputies here, not yet." She looked at Ruie. "I'm going to lock you two in the meat house. So get moving, get over there quick."

"We'll be found there," Ruie said. "Those crooks are out looking for Walt. And they'll be sure to look in the meat house."

"They already have," Easter replied. "It was the first

93

place they searched. And they locked the door when they left. So if they come back there and see the door still locked, they won't search it again. They'll know that even big brother Walt couldn't go inside the meat house, then lock the door from the outside."

"And you wouldn't care if they did find us, would you?" Ruie said.

"I guess I wouldn't. Just so you don't get word to the sheriff about what's happening here." She waved the gun back and forth, pointing it at Ruie's face, then at Dora's. "Move. Those dumb fools are over searching around the henhouse and the straw stack now. I want to have you two locked up safe in the meat house before they start looking over this way."

Easter was slipping the bolt on the meat-house door, pulling the door open, when Ruie said, "You really think you're going to get the ransom money, don't you, Easter?"

"That's my business," Easter said.

"You really think you're clever enough to outsmart Walt, don't you?" Ruie was staring at her.

"Go on inside," Easter said. "I'll take care of big brother Walt, don't you worry about that. I'll kill him if I have to. And if I do, who'll care—the dirty kidnapper?"

Ruie did not move fast enough to suit her, so she gave her a shove, then shoved Dora through the door behind her. "Holler if you feel like it," she said. "Buzz or Gary or one of the girls, or maybe all of them, will hear you if you do. So if you'd rather be their prisoner than mine, just holler."

She closed the door, bolted it. She turned and put her back against it, and looked at the house. There was a chance her father was watching. If he was, she knew he would free Ruie and Dora as soon as she left. There was also a chance that Walt was watching her. There were so many corners, bushes, shadows—hundreds of

94

places to hide. The clear words formed themselves in her mind, "If I could only get Jodie to help me, really help me . . . If he would only listen to reason . . . If he only wasn't so damn honest. . ."

She stood still for a couple of minutes, watching all around, listening deeply. She saw nothing, heard nothing. Suddenly she straightened away from the door, took a deep breath, then walked around the house, keeping to the shadows. She still wore only Jodie's shirt and jacket. Her hair was mussed and tangled; she was sweaty and wanted a bath. She was beginning to be a little hungry, too. She stopped near the gate in the side yard, stood in tree shadow, looked out at the barn, the parked sedans, and the road.

When she got the ransom money, she would leave here in one of those sedans. It was something she had made up her mind she would do; and she hoped Jodie would be driving it. She thought how nice it would be going places, doing things, with Jodie. She liked him more than any fellow she had ever met.

"And he likes me," she told herself. "I'm sure he does. But I'm strange to him. He never knew a girl like me, a girl who didn't give a damn. But he's getting used to me." She thought how, a little while ago, out by the henhouse, he had been against them separating, had wanted them to look for Walt together. He had shown concern for her then, so he did care about her . . . a little, anyway.

Somewhere behind the house, Aggie began shouting, "Buzz! Buzz!" She shouted several times. Easter listened for Buzz to answer. When he finally did, she shrugged, made a wry face. "They're all about half drunk," she told herself, in disgust. "Damn dumb fools. Looking for Walt, a smart cookie like him, and acting like play-party kids on a scavenger hunt. They'll never find him. But he'll find them . . . one at a time. Could be he's

95

already found a couple of them. Damn fools. Walt must have been crazy to get mixed up in a kidnapping with the likes of them."

She was wondering just where Jodie was, and if he had any luck when she heard the front door of the house being opened, heard someone step out on the porch. It was her father, of course. It had to be—he was the only person in the house now. She moved away from the gate, went over to the corner of the house. The porch was all black shadow. She told herself, "It has to be Papa . . . or—" She thought she heard a sound like a car door being closed. She quickly turned around and looked out at the sedans.

Someone was over there. She glimpsed movement, head and shoulders in outline . . . Someone was in between the sedans, had moved a few steps toward the barn. She was peering intently over that way, when a voice behind her said, "I'll take the shortcut across the fields, like you said, Mr. Danson. If they haven't been gone for more than a few minutes, I'll be able to overtake them. I'm sure you did the right thing. I'm worried about Ruie, that's all. But everything's going to be all right. I'll go to town with them. I'll do the talking. I'll make the sheriff understand just how things are here. Don't you worry about that, Mr. Danson."

"My God!" Easter whispered. "Jodie! He thinks he's going after Ruie and Dora—My God! I might have known. He went into the house to fetch Ruie and Dora out, and ran into Papa. I got to stop him. I got to!"

She heard someone walk across the porch, then saw Jodie as he came down the stoop, in the starlight. He was wearing a dark shirt—one of Papa's, Easter thought. "Good night, Mr. Danson," he said; and her father told him good night. He went out by the front gate, turned left, and walked down the lane toward the barn, and the two black sedans.

96

Dora and Ruie sat close together on a bench, their arms around each other, and talking in low tones. Dora was telling Ruie all about herself—her home, her parents. She was an only child. Her parents doted on her, gave her everything she wanted. Last summer she and her mother spent three months in Europe—Paris, Rome, London. It was wonderful. This spring her father had given her a sports car, a Jaguar, for her birthday. Last spring, for her birthday, he had built the swimming pool, where she was swimming when she was kidnapped. She went on and on; then—Ruie did not know exactly when it began—she was crying pitifully.

Ruie did all she could to console her, give her courage. at last she told her about Jodie, how big and handsome and strong and brave he was—about their engagement . . . Jodie's athletic scholarship at Greening U. Dora listened, now and then mumbled some comment, but she did not stop crying—not until they heard someone releasing the bolt on the meat-house door. Then she gave a small, frightened gasp, and was silent.

"It might very well be Papa out here after a slice of ham," Ruie told her. "And it just might be Jodie—it could be Jodie. Let's hope it is."

The door was opened. A flashlight was turned on. Its beam jiggled across the floor, jiggled upward—jerked to a trembling stop on them, on their faces. An instant it was there, blinding them, then it was gone. They heard someone running, going fast toward the house.

"Wh-who was it?" Dora whispered, hugging, clutching Ruie with shaking hands.

"I don't know," Ruie said. "It was a man, I think. The light blinded me so."

"It—it blinded me, too. Why did he run away?"

"Search me," Ruie said. She stood up. "Let's get out of here."

"Are—are we going to that place your father mentioned?"

"Yes," Ruie said. And just then the scream came, high-pitched, wavering, horribly raw with some dreadful emotion—terror, or pain . . .

"That sounded like Papa," Ruie said. "It sounded like it came from out around the barn." She stood still and tense for a moment, listening. The scream did not come again. "I have to go out there," she said. "And you—oh, my God, I don't know what to tell you to do. But I have to go out there. I'm certain it was Papa. He must be in some kind of bad trouble. But you—"

"I'll go with you," Dora said, grabbing her by the hand. "I'll go with you. I'll help you."

They went fast around the corner of the house. They were running in the lane when they heard the moans. The moans were coming from inside the barn. "It is Papa!" Ruie whispered hoarsely. "I know it is."

They found him in the barn, lying in a pile of straw. A flashlight, turned on, lay beside him. They went down on their knees in the straw; Ruie snatched up the light, fixed its beam on his face. "Oh, dear God!" she murmured. Dora, seeing what Ruie saw, made a thin, smacking noise with her lips and sighed.

"Walt did it," Jason Danson said, as Ruie ripped off the tail of her shirt, made a wad of it and wiped the blood off his face. "He knocked me down—kicked me. It happened when I ran out here to try to stop Jodie from going after you two. When I saw you and Dora in the meat house—I was out there after some ham—I knew I had to try to stop him. I didn't want him to go all that way, expecting to find you, then be disappointed. Walt was here—called me inside, asked where you and Dora was. I wouldn't tell him, so he knocked me down, put the boots to me. But I reckon I was more scared than hurt. Who locked you two in the meat house?"

"Easter," Ruie said. "She had a gun, threatened to shoot us. Papa, I don't know what's going to become of Easter. I'm really worried about her."

"So am I," he said. "I'm worried about you, too." He stared at her, and blinked. He looked past her, out through the door, then glanced worriedly at Dora. "You two can't go to Casey Fenser's now," he said. "'Cause likely Walt's on his way over there, and he'd be sure to waylay you and fetch you back. Ruie, you and Dora will have to hide someplace ... in the bull pasture. Old Rub knows you. He won't bother you. And he won't bother Dora so long as she's with you. So that's the place—in the bull pasture, in old Rub's shed. And you two had better hurry. And Jodie—don't worry about him. He came to the house looking for you. I told him where I thought you were—on your way to the Fenser farm. He's got a good start on Walt. I don't think Walt will be able to overtake him."

Ruie nodded. "Are you sure you're all right, Papa?"

"All right enough," Jason said, "to go after Walt, give him the slip and get around him and warn Jodie about this. And that's what I aim to do."

"Be careful, Papa." They went running, then, out to the lane, across the road, across a narrow, weedy field and under the strong, six-strand barbwire fence that surrounded the bull pasture. Here they paused in the shadow of a big tree, to get their breath, and Ruie pointed ahead. "That clump of big trees right over there —old Rub's shed is right behind it. And don't you be afraid if old Rub comes snorting and bellowing around. He won't hurt us. Papa and I raised him from a little calf. I gentled him. He'd likely try to kill anybody else, but he likes me and he likes Papa."

"I—I won't be afraid, no matter what," Dora said. "As long as you're with me, I won't be afraid of anything, Ruie. Honest."

Jodie almost turned back when he heard the scream, but recognized it as a man's, and went on, wondering about it. Then, a short time later, he heard footsteps,

99

someone running behind him. He stopped and turned around. In a few seconds Easter ran out of the shadow of a tree-clump. She saw him and waved, ran faster.

He waited, wanting to curse her. How had she found out he was here, heading for the Fenser farm? Who had told her—not her father, surely. He watched her long, pretty legs flash in the starlight—like living silver, they were. She still wore his shirt and jacket, and nothing else. Both garments were open down the front, and she appeared, oddly, to be running out of them. Her firm breasts bounced ahead of her, buoyantly, as though they knew an urgency of their own, and were eager to reach him.

"Ornery, goofy hussy," he muttered. For a moment he considered running from her, trying to elude her. But he guessed she knew where he was going, and he stood still.

"Jodie!" she gasped, coming to a sudden stop, almost against him. "Jodie, they didn't go to Casey Fenser's place—Ruie and Dora didn't. They started to go there, but Walt caught up with them. He made them go back, Jodie. Jodie, it's the truth! Jodie, I'm not lying this time. Honest!" She was so out of breath she could scarcely speak. She stood, panting, staring at him. She lifted her right hand and crossed her heart with her forefinger.

"How did you know Ruie and Dora started out for the Fenser farm?" he asked, stonily, hating her more than ever he had hated anyone.

"I saw them," she quickly replied. "I was following them. Then Walt stepped out of the shadow of the barn. He had a gun in his hand. He told Ruie they would have to go back. He said—he said, 'I'm going to put you two girls in a good safe place, where you'll keep for a while.' That's exactly what he said, Jodie. S' help me!"

100

"And you followed them to see where he would put them?"

"No. I was going to, but you and Papa came out on the front porch. I saw you. I heard what you both said. Walt and the girls were out of sight then, around the corner of the house. I was in the side yard. I waited till Papa went back inside, then I came after you. I didn't want you running off on a wild-goose chase."

"Well, thanks," he said with heavy sarcasm. "You've got a gun. You might have gone after Walt, made him turn the girls over to you . . . But, oh no, you didn't want to do that, did you?"

She shook her head slowly. "No. I only wanted to come after you, stop you from making a long, useless trip."

He stared at her. He was going to tell her that he still meant to make the trip, to get word to the sheriff about what was going on out here—but he changed his mind, because he suddenly saw that she, not Walt, had stopped Ruie and Dora—that she was holding them prisoners somewhere.

He told himself, "If she'd had a chance to get the drop on Walt, she'd have taken it. She wants the ransom money more than she wants me or anything else. She'd never have given up the opportunity to corner Walt and come after me." All at once, he grinned at her.

She grinned back, showing sudden surprise, "What is it, Jodie?" she asked. "What are you thinking of?"

"You," he said. "Where did you pen them, Easter? Or did you tie them and gag them and leave them lying out in the brush somewhere?"

"Them? Them—who? Who's them you're talking about?"

"Ruie and Dora."

"I—I didn't—"

"You did. You stopped them after they started out to go to the Fenser farm; you didn't kill them. You wouldn't

101

do that. So you tied them up or locked them in. Where are they, in the meat house?"

"Meat house?" She looked away, trilled a weak little laugh, looked quickly back, stared hard into his eyes. "Now wouldn't that be the very place to hide them? Have you forgotten that Buzz, Gary and those two whores are searching the farm, every building, every haystack? How long would anybody stay hidden in the meat house?"

He was still grinning at her. "I got a hunch you locked them in the meat house. I'm going to find out if it's a good hunch."

He stepped around her and struck off through the field, heading back the way he had come. She ran after him. "You wouldn't believe me if I was on my dying bed, gasping my last breath," she said. "So all right, waste your time. Go ahead, look in the meat house."

He did not answer. He was walking so fast, she had to trot to keep up. Once she ran around him, ran backwards in front of him, saying, "I heard a man scream a while ago. I heard Aggie calling Buzz and Buzz answer her just before that. Maybe it was Walt who screamed—maybe Gary and Buzz caught him, were torturing him to make him tell them where he hid the ransom money—" She paused, peered into his face for a moment. "You must have heard the scream."

He nodded. She turned around, slowed her steps and fell in beside him, took hold of his arm with both hands. "I told you the truth, Jodie," she said. "But it might be that Walt locked Ruie and Dora in the meat house."

"Ruie and Dora will know who locked them in there," he said.

"Of course," she replied. She let go of his arm, began buttoning up the shirt.

102

He stopped. "There!" he said. "On the ground in those high weeds. There straight ahead of us—"

She squatted, hands on knees, looking the way he indicated. Suddenly she gasped, "I see it. It—it's somebody—"

He moved on. She went behind him, trying to see around him. "It's a girl!" he said, running faster.

"It's Aggie," she said, as he went down on his knees in the tall weeds. "Is—is she okay, Jodie?"

"I guess so," he mumbled. "Yes—she's all right. She's tied, hands and feet, and gagged."

Easter knelt beside him. Aggie lay on her back, legs bent at the knees, arms beneath her. She was gagged with the panties she had taken from Ruie's suitcase. She was making frantic, *ugg-ugg* noises in her throat. Jodie turned her onto her side. She was tied with clothesline rope, wrists and ankled tied separately.

"Hog-tied," Jodie said. "Walt had me like that, I'd never have made it from the straw stack to the meat house." He told Aggie to be still, then removed the gag. "Who tied you up?" he asked.

"Wa-Wa-Walt!" she rasped, licking her lips rapidly. "He—he chased me and—and Gary. Gary got away, I—I think. He didn't say a word when he c-caught me—hit me in the belly a couple of times, then tied and gagged me when I fell and doubled up. The big, crooked bastard!"

"Is that all you can tell us about him?"

"Yeah." She blinked at Jodie. "Who're you? I never seen you before."

"Never mind who I am. Do you know anything about Ruie and Dora?"

She waggled her head, still blinking at him. "They ain't in the house. There ain't nobody in the house. Gary and I was in there a little while ago. It was when we come out and started down to the barn that Walt took after us."

"Mr. Danson must be in the house."

She waggled her head again. "Nope. Nobody in the house."

"Do you know anything about Buzz and Emma?"

"Not now. We was all out looking for Walt. It was Buzz's idea. He thought maybe we could catch him, make him hand over the ransom money. Hell of an idea, that was. Awhile ago I got lost from Gary—it was out by the straw stack. I thought I heard Buzz say something to Emma. I couldn't see anybody around. I yelled to Buzz and he answered me. Gary found me right then. I—I don't know where Buzz and Emma are now. I don't know where Gary is, either."

Jodie pushed the panties back into her mouth.

She chewed them out again, cursed him. "You going to gag me again!—" she cried. "You going to leave me here! Goddamn you! Wa—Walt'll come back and kill me! He knows you're here. He saw you two coming just as he finished tying me. He ran, but he saw you first."

Jodie shoved the panties past her teeth, tried to hold them there. She fought him, tried to bite his fingers, until Easter grabbed big handfuls of hair and banged her head on the ground. "Let him gag you, whore! You hear! You want me to bump your brains out in the dirt!"

Jodie tied the gag in place. He and Easter stood up. He said to Aggie, "Somebody'll come and untie you when the sheriff gets here." He looked at Easter. Aggie was making the *ugg-ugg* noise again. Easter gave him a loose grin.

He moved off toward the house. She followed him, her right hand in the jacket pocket. They were passing the corner of the barn before either of them spoke again. Then Easter said, "Walt's got some idea he's trying to work out, tying up and gagging people like he's doing. He came back here for only one thing—I'm sure of that much. He came back here to get rid of everybody who knows he helped kidnap Dora—everybody who might

104

give him away to the law, that is. I don't think he means to kill Papa."

"He's not loony," Jodie replied. "He wouldn't kill so many. Besides, he had a chance to kill me and Aggie and Gary, and we're all still alive."

"Gary might not be alive," Easter replied. "And maybe Walt wants to kill them some way that'll make it look like they died by accident, like in a fire. He's got some plan he's trying to work out. I know that big heel. I know him better than anybody else. In lots of ways we're alike, we think the same way."

Jodie said nothing, but he believed part of what she said—the part about her and Walt being alike. They stopped in the lane, stood in the tree shadow for a moment and looked at the house. They listened. The living-room windows showed light through drawn blinds. The other windows were dark.

Suddenly Jodie started on. Easter went after him, walking close at his heels. She still had her right hand in the jacket pocket. She said as they passed through the gate in the side yard, "If Papa's not in the house or close around it somewhere, then something bad must have happened to him. Do you reckon Aggie told us the truth?"

"Yes," Jodie replied.

They did not pause again or speak until they reached the meat house. Then Easter, standing close behind Jodie as he unlocked the door, put the muzzle of Gary Summerfield's gun against his back. He stiffened slightly, went on with what he was doing, not looking at her— slipped the bolt, pulled the door open.

"I—I got the guts to kill you, to kill anybody!" she whispered.

"Ruie," he said, peering into the darkness. "Ruie, it's Jodie—"

There was no answer, only a rustling, a heavy breathing, a faint moaning. He moved inside fast, stooping low, feeling out and down in front of him. Easter stayed right behind him, tried to keep the gun against him, but could not. He felt of the floor as he went, felt a human face suddenly, and stopped—a nose, eyes, a mouth with a gag in it under his exploring fingers.

"My God!" he said. At that moment Easter was able to put the gun against his back again.

"They're not in here!" she gasped. "I—I didn't tie them. Besides—oh, God, Jodie, this is a man! I feel his shoe!"

He straightened up. "I'll drag him out in the light," he said. His voice shook.

"I—I hid them—Ruie and Dora," Easter said. "But I didn't tie them. I—"

"Hid them in here, you mean?" He turned, grabbed her, jerked her up against him. "Answer me, Easter, or by God I'll—"

"N-no! No! . . . I hid them somewhere else. They're safe there. Honest to God, Jodie, I didn't hurt them! I'll go and turn them loose just as soon as I can find Walt and make him tell me where he hid the ransom money. They were on their way to the Fenser farm to get Casey Fenser to drive them to town. I had to stop them. If the sheriff and his deputies come out here, I'll never get the ransom money—never even get a chance at it. Can't you understand? I've got to have that money! I've got to get away from here—from this rat-trap. I'll go stark, raving crazy if I don't. You don't know what it's been like, cooped up here in the wilderness with an old man—a cranky old man—my father. If he wasn't my father, maybe it wouldn't have been so bad— even an old man like him. But, Jodie, I've got to get away from here! I've got to get that money!"

He let her go, stooped over, felt until he had solid hand-holds on the bound man's ankles. He began to tug, walking backwards. "Another of Walt's victims," he muttered. "Gary or Buzz, likely. He's gagged and tied the same as Aggie."

106

Moments later, out in the starlight, he saw he had guessed right. The bound man was Gary Summerfield.

He looked at Easter, who still held the gun in her hand and said, "No use taking the gag out, I reckon. Best to drag him back inside, leave him where we found him."

Gary heard this and began wriggling around, grunting, chewing his gag. Jodie and Easter watched him for a moment, then Jodie squatted and removed the gag, which had been made from a sleeve of Gary's shirt. "All right, you wanted to talk, now talk," he said.

Gary had not had the gag in his mouth very long. It was not difficult for him to speak. "Walt and I fought," he said, looking up at Easter. "He—he slug—slugged me. When I came to I was in there, like you found me. Easter—Easter honey, Walt's a madman. You just don't know. He's going to kill us all. Please, Easter, help me, make your friend help me!" He glanced at Jodie.

"Where's Buzz and Emma?" Jodie asked.

Gary shook his head. "You kidding me, mister?" He gave Easter a puzzled, inquiring look. "Buzz is in there, tied and gagged," he said. "I thought you found him. He's conscious."

"My God, Walt got both of 'em!" Easter exclaimed. "By now he's likely got Emma, got her hog-tied somewhere, like he's got Aggie. Next he'll come after you and me, Jodie!"

Gary, staring up at her, eagerly nodded. "You're dead right, Easter honey," he said. "Walt's going to kill us all, the whole kit and boodle of us. So please help me, Easter honey! We're old friends. You used to like me a lot. Remember how it was between us, Easter honey?"

"Gag the bastard and we'll drag him back in the meat house," Easter said, and looked all around. "Hurry, we got to find Walt before he jumps us, fixes us like he did these two and Aggie. Hurry."

107

They placed Gary as far away from his friend as they possibly could, then went outside.

"It's okay," Easter said, as Jodie closed and bolted the door. "Even if they manage to untie each other, they can't get out. This place is built like a tomb. Double walls, concrete under the floor. Papa did a good job here. Meat stays cool and dry, never gets moldy."

"Easter," Jodie said, turning and taking her arm, "you're going to tell me what you did with Ruie and Dora. Do you understand? I'll beat it out of you if I have to."

"I've got a gun," she replied.

He gave a mirthless chuckle. "I'm not afraid of your gun. I'd have taken it, only I figured you needed it for your own protection. You wouldn't shoot me. You like me and I like you. That's why you're going to tell me where Ruie and Dora are, because you like me, and I like you. . . ."

She was silent for a moment, gazing into his eyes. "You like me, but you're in love with Ruie."

"People change," he said. "Ruie could have tried to help me instead of taking Dora and trying to run away, to Casey Fenser's place. It's like she thought getting away from here, getting the law to come here, was more important than staying here, trying to give me a hand. It's like she ran out on me. I've been thinking about it, the way she acted. Don't think I haven't."

"Ruie's no coward," Easter said, her tone speculative, suspicious. "She might not be as deep in love with you as you thought, but she's no coward."

"That's what I mean," he replied. "If she was as much in love with me as I am with her, she wouldn't have tried to leave without making sure I was all right. I didn't mean that she's a coward. If it was that, if she tried to leave here because she was afraid . . . well, I wouldn't hold that against her."

"No—no, I guess you wouldn't, Jodie."

He watched her face for some sign that she was suspicious of his pretended change of feeling toward Ruie; but there was nothing to see. Yet his suspicions grew—it was like she had been expecting him to say what he had just said. So either she believed he really cared for her more than for Ruie, or else she was pretending the way he was—stalling, not wanting to tell him where she had hidden Ruie and Dora, and dreading to have to face up to a beating.

He guessed she believed his threat about the beating—he guessed she did—but what a liar she was. He glanced at the house. "I guess we ought to go in the house and take a second look around," he said.

"Why so?" She seemed suddenly alarmed—glanced at the house, then looked at him, her eyes very wide. "You can beat up on me out here as well as in there."

"Your father may be in there, hurt. Walt may be in there. We're looking for Walt, remember?"

She nodded. "I don't want to see Papa ever again," she said. "I—I just want to go away from here, far away from here, and stay away from here."

He tugged at her arm. "Come on, we're going in the house."

She did not say anything. He gave another tug. She loosened up, came with him. "I wanted to kill you a while ago," she said, "when I told you not to look for Ruie in the meat house and you wouldn't listen. I wanted to kill you, really I did; and I didn't chicken out or anything like that, either. I didn't kill you because I'm in love with you. I want us to leave here together, stay together forever."

"You mean if we find the ransom money," he said. "You don't mean for us to leave here right now?"

"Yes," she said. "Right now. I've already found the ransom money. I found it a few minutes after Walt hit you in the head with the rock. It's the truth. I'll show it

109

to you—if you'll prove to me that you care more about me than you do about Ruie."

He laughed flatly, staring into her eyes, where the starlight shone the color of old, clean pewter. "You're the one biggest liar in the whole world," he said. "If you had the money you wouldn't have it here—you'd be long gone with it by now."

She nodded, looking at him steadily as they halted by the kitchen door. "I can't drive. I have the keys for one of those sedans. I took them from Gary when I took his gun and wallet. I hid them with the money. But I can't drive. Of course, I could ask Gary or Buzz to drive for me—but I guess you wouldn't stand for that."

She smiled at him, moved against him and put her arms around him. "I want you to drive for me, Jodie," she whispered, slowly moving her belly against him, slowly rubbing, pinching his buttocks with her small, soft, strong fingers.

He stood still for a long moment, not really wanting her, but thinking about taking her—wondering if she would be different from Ruie, from any other girl. He never had taken any other girl, only Ruie. He never had planned on taking any other girl. He was in love with Ruie. He firmly believed he would always be in love with Ruie.

He said, finally, "I'll tell you what, I'll prove to you that I care more for you than for Ruie—if you'll first tell me where you hid Ruie and Dora. I promise. I have to know that Ruie's safe and okay. When I'm sure of that, then I'll do anything you want."

"Drive away from here in Gary's sedan with me, you'll do that?"

"Yes," he lied. "But not right away. My head hurts. I'm hungry. I need rest."

"Make love to me first, here—in the house, in my bedroom?"

"Yes," he said, not knowing if it was a lie or not.

110

"Okay!" she said eagerly. "Come on. Oh, I hope Aggie was right! I hope there is no one in the house. I want to wash myself first, comb my hair—"

"No," he said, grabbing her as she twisted away from him, turning toward the door. "First you tell me where Ruie and Dora are."

"I—I won't! We make love first. That's the way it's got to be, Jodie."

8

WALT squatted and laid the flashlight on the meathouse floor, then set the lantern down beside it and struck a match. The sudden upward glow cut his big, flat face in half—the big, shallow, pale eyes and broad, low, deeply wrinkled forehead in yellow light, the large, hooked nose and long, slit mouth in near darkness.

He lit the lantern, picked up the flashlight, turned it off, put it in his jacket pocket. Then he squinted across the lantern at the five tied and gagged people lying on the floor. He grinned and ran the tip of his tongue all the way around his mouth.

He said, "I collected the ransom. I got away. I wasn't followed. Everything went just as I planned. And, fool me, I came here tonight intending to make the three-way divvy. And what did I find?"

He lifted a hand and pointed at Emma, then at Aggie. "I found those two no-good whores, that's what I found." He looked at Buzz, then at Gary, and his thin, twitching grin faded. "I told you guys not to let anybody else in on this. I even warned you, told you what I'd do to you. But along came a couple of hot-tailed chippies, and—Well, when I saw those two tarts here, I changed my mind. I decided to do away

111

with the lot of you. So I hid the money and got busy."

He looked at them all, glared at them one by one, then rose and went and took the gag from Gary Summerfield's mouth. "You can do the talking, Gary," he said. "We're old buddies. We've known each other all our lives. When I think about killing the five of you, you're the only one I have any qualms about. You can do the talking." He went back and squatted where he had been, stared at Gary. "Where's the money, Gary? Did you find it? You tell me where it is, Gary, and maybe I'll let you stay alive."

Gary licked his lips, opened his mouth wide, closed it slowly. He did this several times before he said, "Easter was here and a guy I never saw before was with her. They ungagged me. We talked a little. I didn't tell them anything. It was after you brought Buzz in; so Easter and the guy know Buzz and I are here. They're probably watching this place from the dark. Could be, Walt, you shouldn't have come in here. Another thing, it wasn't so smart to close the door behind you. Somebody could of slipped up out there and slipped the bolt over and nobody in here would've heard it. Could be you're locked in here with the rest of us right now."

Walt Danson appeared to pay no attention. He did not even glance back at the closed door. He stared at Gary and said, "Did you find the money, Gary? If you didn't, who did? You don't tell me, you'll croak with the others here."

"Ain't you even going to see if the door's locked?" Gary asked.

"No. If it's locked, its' locked. That guy with Easter was Ruie's husband-to-be. He's in the house with Easter. Ruie's tied up and locked in our bullshed. My papa wouldn't lock me in here. He's the only one here I can trust. So don't you worry about the door, Gary. You just tell me who got the money out from under

112

the straw in that setting-hen's nest out in the henhouse, where I hid it."

"I didn't," Gary said, looking surprised, glancing around at the others. "Maybe Easter got it. She's been outside here ever since we came."

Walt shook his head. "I told you, Easter's in the house with Ruie's boy friend. She wouldn't be there, or anyplace else around here, if she had the money. It was one of you that got it, not counting little richy-bitchy Dora over there." He glanced at Dora Shetsher, who was staring at him, eyes wide with fear. He grinned at her. "She was out in the bullshed with Ruie," he said. "I had to carry her all the way over here. She wouldn't walk, and she fought me every step of the way—put up a better fight than any of you." He sneered around at them, at Gary last.

Gary shrugged. "I ain't got the money, Walt," he said. "I don't know who has got it, either. You better talk to the others."

Walt glared at him for a moment, then looked at Buzz. "How about you?" he said.

Buzz grunted, chewed his gag, and shook his head.

Walt looked at Emma, then Aggie, got a headshake from both of them.

He swore under his breath and stood up. "There's a manure pit out behind the cow stable," he said. "I reckon the way to get the proper cooperation out of you damn-fool liars is to drag you out there and throw you in it. Tied up like you are, and deep and soft as that stuff is in the pit, you'll drown if somebody doesn't get you out pretty quick. And one thing, sure as apples don't grow on pea vines, I won't get you out if you don't tell me what I want to know."

He looked at them all, one at a time, then shrugged his massive shoulders. "I meant to get you all in here and blast you to death with a couple of sticks of Papas' stump-bustin' dynamite," he said. "But I reckon you'll

113

be just as dead if you strangle to death on rain-water and manure." He shrugged again, turned and went to the door.

"I'll take you out first, Aggie," he said, and shoved on the door.

The door did not move. "Must be stuck," he muttered, shoving on it again, harder. Still the door did not move. He swore a harsh oath, put his shoulder against it, gave a powerful, lunging shove. The door did not move. He stood back, swore again, turned and looked at Gary.

"I told you," Gary said. "That Easter is as sly and watchful as a fox. I told you, didn't I?"

"Yes," Walt said. He walked over and stood in front of Gary. "Yes, you did tell me." And he kicked Gary deliberately in the face.

"I told you how it happened, Papa," Ruie was saying impatiently. "Walt saw Dora and me in the bull pasture. He opened the gate, threw rocks at old Rub till old Rub ran out in the road, then he crawled under the fence, closed the gate, and came on out to old Rub's shed—tied me, left me in the shed, and brought Dora over here."

Jason Danson shook his head, wonderingly. "That Walt's a sharp one, all right. But he sure cooked his own goose this time, letting old Rub out in the road that way. 'Cause I was cutting the buck down the road, thinking I was following him, and not aiming to turn back till I came up with him—then I see old Rub coming down the road after me. Right then I knew something was bad wrong. I knew you wouldn't leave the gate open, and I knew old Rub wouldn't come out if you did, but would follow you like he always does. Besides, that bull's dangerous, so I couldn't let him go astray. So I drove him back to pasture. Then I see Walt carrying the Shetsher girl around the house, and something told me you was out in the bullshed and in a bad fix. So I hustled my stumps right on out there, and—"

"Papa, please don't explain about it any more," Ruie interrupted him. "It's not important now, Papa. Walt didn't hurt me. Old Rub's back in his pasture. Papa, I think we ought to try to find out who's in the house. We know somebody is. We saw the kitchen blinds being pulled down."

Jason shook his head. "I don't think so," he said. "Luck's been running with us this last hour or so. So let's not push it."

"Well, we just can't stay around outside forever, Papa," Ruie said.

They had come out to the straw stack after Jason had sneaked in from the road and bolted the meat-house door, after Walt had carried Dora inside and closed it. Now they concealed themselves in the stack's shadow and watched the house, hoping whoever was in it would come out. They knew others besides Walt and Dora were in the meat house, but they did not know who they were. Jason believed Walt had turned back before overtaking Jodie, and that by now Casey Fenser was driving Jodie to town to call on the sheriff. He also believed there were two people in the house— Gary and Aggie. He did not now why he believed this; he just did. He had told Ruie of these beliefs of his; now, suddenly, he was telling her of them further.

"I got a notion every last single soul of us and them, 'cept you and me and Gary and Aggie—including Easter, too—is locked in the meat house," he said. "And if that's so, then all we have to do is wait. Pretty soon Gary and Aggie will come out of the house and start looking around, and—well, maybe I can sneak up on Gary and hit him in the head with a rock or something, and you and me can tackle Aggie. Then we'll have them all, and all we'll have to do is settle back and wait for Sheriff Bjornson to get here."

115

"But, Papa, suppose Jodie didn't make it to the Fenser place? We can't be sure he did, just because he left here to go there. Walt went after Ruie and me when he thought we were on our way to the Fenser place, so he might have run into Jodie, done something to him. Jodie might be in the meat house right now with the others. And we're not sure who's in the house. Just because you saw Gary and Aggie in the yard, doesn't mean they went in the house. Papa, we just can't wait and do nothing."

"Walt didn't know Jodie was on his way to the Fensers'," Jason said. "He somehow knew you and Dora started out to go there, or maybe he guessed it. When I saw you and Dora in the meat house and ran out front to try to overhaul Jodie, and Walt met me at the barn, he didn't ask about Jodie. He only accused me of turning Dora loose and having you take her some place. He grabbed me and shoved me in the barn. He cussed me and said I sent you and Dora to the Fenser place, but he'd stop you from ever getting there. Then he knocked me down and kicked me, and I yelled. I didn't see him leave. But I don't see how he could have caught up with Jodie. He didn't have time. He was back here too soon. It's my notion he was still around and saw you and Dora when you came running to the barn after I yelled. So I wouldn't worry about Jodie not getting through to the Fenser place, if I was you."

"Well, I am worried about him," Ruie replied. "And I think we had best find out for certain who's in the house. Papa, I—I want to sneak over to the house and try to peek in at a window. I won't go inside, honest. I'll just try to see inside, through a window."

"No. I think it's best that we wait right here for a while. If Gary and Aggie come out and it looks like they might be going to let Walt and the others out of the meat house by accident, we can stop them. I can holler

116

and tell them that Walt's in there, and they won't open the door, you betcha."

"No," Ruie said, "they'll come running out here. Papa, we wouldn't stand a chance trying to fight Gary and Aggie. Papa, are you forgetting your age? Besides, you're hurt. And you need attention, too—the proper kind. Those cuts and bruises on your face need bathing with hot water and plenty of soap. Papa, I'm going over and try to find out who's in the house. I am! And I don't want you to come with me."

He stared at her for a moment, then nodded. "All right, have it your way. But if Gary and Aggie get you, I'm going to let Walt out of the meat house. He's dead set on putting an end to the lot of them, but I don't figure he'll kill us, you and me and Easter, his own flesh and blood. I hate to think of Dora being killed, but if Gary Summerfield gets you, I'm going to turn Walt loose so he can get Gary Summerfield."

"Gary won't get me," Ruie said. "I don't think Gary's in the house. I think he's in the meat house. I think Walt caught them all, and they're all in the meat house."

"Then who do you figure is in the house?"

"Easter," she said. "And—and Jodie."

"Well, you're dead wrong," old Jason said, then spat emphatically. "You might be right about it being Easter in the house, but that boy friend of yours is likely just about now driving into town with Casey Fenser in Casey's old jeep. But you go ahead, have it your way. Go peek in the windows. But if Gary gets you, I'm going to turn your brother loose. You can depend on that."

Easter had locked the doors and fastened the windows, pulled the window blinds that were not pulled already. She had blown out all the lamps, except the one in the kitchen. That one she had set on the kitchen table, put Gary Summerfield's little .32 automatic on the table beside it. Then she had rekindled the fire in the cookstove, heated water, made coffee, warmed over some cold fried ham and mashed potatoes she had found in the pantry.

While the food was warming, the coffee making, she had poured hot water into a big tin wash basin, bathed Jodie's hurts, rubbed liniment on his bruises, put iodine on his cuts.

She had washed his face and hands, arms and chest, while he sat in a chair beside the kitchen table. Then she had taken a fresh basin of hot water, soap, a clean, dry towel, had gone into the dark living room and bathed herself. After that she had gone upstairs to her room and put on a clean house dress, a pale red one that fit her loosely.

It was almost four o'clock when they ate the ham and potatoes, and some dried-out cake she had found in the cupboard. Outside, the birds were beginning to chirrup drowsily. It was still dark, but that was because dawn was dimming the stars. Daylight would soon be taking over.

All this while, for nearly an hour, Jodie had been protesting, aloud to her, silently to himself. He had said many times that they should be watching the meat house, that Walt would return there, fetch Aggie and Emma, and that they could take him with the gun, if they were out there, waiting, watching.

Also, he had asked her dozens of times to tell him where she had hidden Ruie and Dora—had threatened to beat her if she did not tell him. He had brought up her father to her, too, told her he might be outside somewhere hurt, even dying.

But all he had said, his pleas, his threats, had seemed to make no impression on her. And now as they finished eating, he was wondering if he was not the coward she had called him, if he was not a spineless, no-good slob. . . .

When he thought of all that had happened during the

118

past several hours, it seemed unreal, like unrelated incidents recalled from a dream. All those people running around, searching, hiding, out there in the pale darkness. And it was difficult for him to place himself in the pictures which kept forming in his memory, letting him see the mistakes he had made, know the moments when he should have acted—when he should have jumped Gary—Buzz—when he should not have permitted Easter to intimidate him.

For one thing, he should have gone on to the Fenser place. He should not have believed Easter and turned back. If he had gone on, the sheriff and his deputies would be here now, probably.

"And when I knew Easter was such a goofy liar," he told himself. He put down his coffee cup, looked across the table. He winced as Easter smiled at him.

"I got to be really mad before I can just—just hurt a person," he said. "I—I can't just up and bash somebody, not unless I lose my temper. I ought to have stomped Gary's head to a pulp when I found him out there in the meat house a while ago—for what he did, tried to do to Ruie. I thought about it. I wanted to kick his teeth out. But he was tied. I couldn't do it. I guess I'm what you called me once—a—a piss-willie."

Easter shook her head. "You got plenty of guts, Jodie," she said. "You're just young and inexperienced. You never run up against anything like this before. I never did either, but I—I'm different from you. I had to get tough early. Guys after me all the time, trying to get me to—to do it with them, fighting me to get me to do it . . . I was raped three times. Did I tell you?"

He stared at her, licked his lips. "No," he said. Then, shaking his head, he mumbled, "My God!"

She laughed softly. "It wasn't so bad. It didn't hurt too much, and it didn't get me pregnant. I figure I was lucky."

"A pretty girl has it tough, I guess." He went on staring at her, licking his lips.

She nodded. "Around here, the kind of stupid clods I've had to associate with, any girl would have it tough."

He thought of Ruie, wondered how tough she had had it here. He said, "Easter, I'm not going to wait much longer. You promised to tell me where you had Ruie and Dora. Easter, I don't want to have to hurt you to make you tell me."

She went on smiling. "You promised to make love to me, remember?" she said. "I'll keep my promise when you keep yours."

He stared at her. "I don't want to make love now," he said. "A fellow can't just make love any old time. I told you, later—when I'm sure Ruie is okay, then we can make love. I'll want to do it then."

"With Ruie?" She gave a quick little laugh.

"No. Easter, I told you, I'll drive you away from here. All I want is to know that Ruie is okay."

He knew he was lying, yet it seemed, strangely, that he did not know it for sure. It was almost as if he had truly decided to drive her away, to do what she wanted him to do. He was tired and hurt, that was what was the matter. He was not thinking clearly; he just was not himself. After he got a little sleep, then he would be all right. He was not going to drive her away. He was not going to make love to her. He had only told her he would do those things so she would tell him where she had hidden Ruie and Dora. But how did he know for certain that she had hidden Ruie and Dora? She had lied about so many other things . . . So how could he afford to believe her about this?

It was all so useless, so crazy. At first things had seemed to make sense, but now—He was to blame. Those blows on the head. They had left him fuzzy, he guessed. Because there had been a kidnapping . . . Walt had collected the ransom, then come on here to kill

Gary and Buzz so he would not have to share the ransom ... That made sense. Walt had not expected to find Aggie and Emma here, nor Ruie, nor himself.

Walt had set out to capture his friends one at a time, then kill them all at the same time. And he had done it. That is, he had captured the four of them—at least, it seemed that he had. Aggie bound and gagged out in the field, Gary and Buzz bound and gagged in the meat house ... And he had captured Emma, too, of course. And now, or very soon, he would have them all imprisoned in the meat house. Was that where he was going to kill them, in the meat house? And how about Dora Shetsher, had he captured her, too? And how about Ruie?

Easter finished the coffee in her cup. She stood up, looking at him. "You're worried about Ruie, and I'm worried about Walt," she said. "He won't just go away and leave the ransom money behind, you know. He'll stay until he finds it, or until something happens to stop him looking. Sooner or later he's going to try to get in here, and when he does, I'm going to shoot him."

"You won't shoot him," Jodie told her. "You're just talking. You haven't got the ransom money. You lied about that. You lied about everything. You don't know where Ruie and Dora are." He stood up, walked around the table and stood in front of her. "I'm through listening to you, trying to believe your lies. I'm going outside. I'm going to find out how many tied-up people there are in the meat house now."

He started toward the door. She ran and got in front of him. She put her hands flat against his chest and shoved. "Wait!" she whispered. "I've been trying and trying to think of the best thing to do. I have lied to you, plenty. But I do have the money. I do know where Ruie and Dora are. I—I locked them in—inside somewhere. I won't tell you where till you—you—till I'm sure you're on my side. But they're safe. They can't

121

get out, but they're okay. I—I've been thinking—why should I be afraid of the law—I hid the money in a place nobody will ever find it. I wasn't in on the kidnapping. I haven't done anything so bad, nothing the sheriff will want to lock me up for. So why should I be afraid? I think Papa went to Casey Fenser's house, and he and Casey went to town to get the sheriff, but— well, I've got the money, and I can keep it. I—I'm going to keep it. If Walt tries to break in here and I shoot him —well, he's a kidnapper. Papa, even Ruie and Dora Shetsher, even you—all of you will have to stand by me. See what I mean? See what I'm getting at, Jodie? I don't have to worry about the law. I don't have to worry about anything or anybody, only just my big brother Walt."

He nodded, staring hard into her eyes. Then he grabbed her, clutched her shoulders, shook her until her head snapped, until she cried out. "You have to worry about me!" he shouted. "You have to tell me where Ruie and Dora are! You have to do that, and right now!"

"Jodie!" she cried. "Jodie, for God's sake!"

His head was going around and around, and there was a big, mean buzzing inside it. He could not see so good, either. He knew, in a way, that he was strangling Easter. He knew his hands on her throat had stopped her yelling. He knew he had to go on strangling her until she told him where Ruie was. He knew—

She was hitting him, clawing at him. Then, suddenly, she had her arms and legs around him, and he was staggering around the table with her. He saw his hands on her throat. He saw down between his wrists, saw her big smooth breasts there, pumping out under the torn dress. He felt her thighs squeezing his hips, her warm belly pressing against him. He went around the table with her, all the way around, and, all at once, he said to himself, "I'm killing her. I'm killing her." In the

122

next instant he was telling himself, "Don't lose your temper. You've got a mean temper. Don't lose it. Don't lose your temper . . ."

He let go of her throat. "My God!" he said. "My God, I killed her!"

He put his arms around her, and she went limp. He gathered her up in his arms like a baby and ran out of the kitchen, through the dining room, through the living room. He ran up the stairs. It was dark. He stumbled twice, almost fell. He found the door to Easter's room, kicked it open. He ran through it, ran against the bed, fell—fell on the bed with Easter in his arms—under him in his arms.

She was limp and motionless. He lay still for a moment, not breathing, listening to know if she was breathing. Finally he jerked his head down, pushed her soft breasts apart with his face, turned his head and pressed his ear hard against her. He heard her heart. He thought he did—She sighed. She was breathing! She was not dead! He had not killed her!

"Thank God!" he said.

Downstairs, grabbing her, shaking her, strangling her, he had ripped her dress down the front to below her waist. Now it was like she was naked under him. She stirred. Her thighs twitched, and he realized he was in between them. He started to get off her. "Easter," he said. "Easter, are you all right?"

She stirred again, sighed again. Her breasts rose hard against him. She needs something, he thought. "Smelling salts—" he murmured. But there would be no smelling salts in this house. Camphor, then—Or whiskey. There was a bottle downstairs, left in the kitchen by one of the kidnappers. Perhaps there was some whiskey in it.

"I'll get you something," he said. "I'll get you some whiskey." He was getting off her as he spoke. She sighed, stirred, but did not speak. He scrambled off the bed and ran out in the hall, ran downstairs.

123

The bottle contained two big swallows of whiskey. He snatched it off the sideboard, ran back upstairs with it, stumbling twice, cursing the darkness. "I should have brought the lamp along," he told himself, entering Easter's room. "Damn fool me," he mumbled, and kneeled on the bed.

She was lying just as he had left her—in the darkness on her back, legs spread slightly. He felt over her quickly, slipped his hand under her head, lifted it up, put the bottle to her lips. "Easter—Easter—" he muttered. "Easter, I'm sorry! I didn't want to hurt you. Honest!"

She stirred, turned her head away. He tried to follow her mouth with the bottle, but could not. It was too dark. She muttered unintelligibly. He got his knees between her legs. He almost let her head fall as she turned it still farther away. He got a new fix for his hand, lifted her head higher. She went on muttering. He got the mouth of the bottle against her lips. She gave her head a hard shake. He dropped the bottle, heard it hit the floor behind the bed, and roll.

"It was whiskey," he said.

She was still muttering. He started to move from between her legs, thinking to get the bottle, hoping all the whiskey was not lost. Her legs moved, locked themselves around his legs. She moaned and struggled up, and put her arms around him.

"No!" he gasped. "I—I won't. No! Easter, I want to be true to Ruie. Easter, I won't! Goddamn you to hell! Easter!"

She was tearing his shirt with her teeth. She was beating him with her pelvis, twisting, flouncing, rocking her hips. "Easter, for—Easter, don't!"

She held him hard with her legs, jerked an arm from around him, grabbed at him, grabbed his pants, jerked on them, went on jerking on them, and making tight, small, harsh, squealing noises in her throat. "No!" he gasped.

He thought of slugging her. He could. He could get away from her, all right. He could grab her and overpower her and get away from her. He did grab her, by the shoulders, shoved her back on the bed. His pants flew open at the fly as he did so.

He drew up his legs, got his knees on the bed, lunged upward. She grabbed him with both arms, held on to him. He twisted around, got a foot on the floor. "I won't!" he cried.

And just then the slats in the bed jumped their rails and struck the floor with a loud banging and clattering. The springs and mattress dropped down inside the steads and the rails, and he and she dropped down with them.

She was after his pants with both hands. She had ruined the zipper. Suddenly, she began pushing them down, tugging and shoving at them. Her hands were on his flesh. He knocked her hands away, got up on to his knees. She came up after him, quickly, threw her arms around him. He jerked himself backwards to break her hold, and his hip struck the bed rail. He swore, threw himself forward and tried to get his feet under him. She pulled him toward her, fell back—and the toe of his shoe caught on the mattress cover. He tried to kick it loose, and fell on top of her.

"Oh, Jodie!" she gasped. "Oh, Jodie!"

"I—I won't!" he moaned, finding it difficult to get his breath, the crumpled twisted position he was in. "I love Ruie. I'm going to be true to Ruie. I won't!"

"Oh, Jodie!"

He was trying to get on to his knees. She held on to him with arms and legs. He almost made it. Their faces bumped. Her lips seemed to clutch at his lips. She kissed him with her whole mouth, lips, tongue.

In the next instant he was taking off his pants and she was helping him. He was murmuring, saying things

125

he did not understand himself. She was doing the same. "Th-the damn old bed had to—to go—to go and fall down!" he whispered.

"Yeah, the damn old bed had—had to—to—to go and fall—fall—damn old—" she whispered. Her fingers crept up between his legs, and this time he did not try to stop them. He groaned with pleasure, his body arching, muscles going tight. His own hands were busy, finding the soft naked curves of her thighs and buttocks, squeezing them, pulling her closer to him.

She whispered again. "And—and fall down," she said. They were clutching, stroking, pulling at each other's bodies. Jodie's head dipped as if by itself, and he was nuzzling her big, firm breasts like a calf, his lips hunting for the nipples. He found them, sucked and pulled at them with his mouth, while she moaned and clutched his back. And somehow the swollen ache of him was sliding into her warm softness that shaped itself around his flesh, and as he began to move, she said, "Oh! Oh my! Oh, Jodie! Lover!"

9

"HOW in the world did it ever happen, Ruie?" he asked, panting, rubbing perspiration off his face and neck with his hands. "I thought for sure you were Easter until you kissed me—then I knew. But how did it ever happen? How did you get here in Easter's room? And where's Easter?"

Ruie was having too difficult a time getting her breath to really laugh. But she tried. Even if she had managed, it would not have been a happy laugh.

"The goofy little slut," she said, and paused, panting.

"She's goofy all right," Jodie said. "But—but where is she?"

"I—I don't know," Ruie told him. "Could be she's down in the back yard. I slugged her. I—I did, really. Jodie, I—I slugged her. I—I hit her in the face about—about a dozen times. I really gave her everything I had—right in the face."

"Y-you and Easter fought?"

"She didn't; I did. The dirty little crackpot!"

"What did you do to her, Ruie? Where is she?"

Ruie did not answer immediately. Finally she asked, "Do you really care, Jodie?"

"Care for Easter—like her as a—as a girl—as a girl for me? My God, no! But where is she?"

"I told you where she might be. Down in the back yard—if the fall down the porch roof knocked her unconscious. If it didn't, or if it did and she came to, she might be anywhere. I rolled her up in the bed covers and pillows and shoved her out the window and rolled her off the porch roof. I did that after I slugged her. I don't know whether I knocked her out or not. But I gave her everything I had."

"You came in here through the window off the porch roof, while I was downstairs getting the whiskey—"

"Yes," Ruie said. "But I was outside the window listening before that. I knew when you brought her up here. I heard everything you said. And don't think for a second that I didn't know what she was up to—acting like she had fainted or something—I got wise to her little tricks, and big ones, too, a long, long time ago."

"I strangled her to make her tell me where she had you and Dora locked up," Jodie said. "I did it downstairs in the kitchen, and I thought I had killed her. I carried her up here and—"

"She was only pretending to be unconscious," Ruie interrupted. "As soon as you went downstairs to get the whiskey, she got up, took off what was left of her clothes, lay down again and fixed herself, got ready."

"Is that the truth?"

"It certainly is the truth. I was right outside the window. I had Papa's flashlight, and when she got herself all fixed for you, I climbed in through the window. She was breathing so hard from the struggle with you downstairs that she didn't hear me. I turned on the light and there she was, just like I knew she would be. Naked. Waiting for you. Oh, I just fairly boiled. I jumped onto her. I pulled her off the bed. I slugged her. I wanted to kill the dirty little hussy."

"I—I don't blame you," Jodie said. He put his arms around her, kissed her on the neck. "I love you, Ruie."

"I'm sorry I tricked you like that," she murmured. "I—I guess I'm as ornery as Easter when—when you're the fellow."

"You're just as good as my wife right now," he told her, and kissed her. She kissed him back.

"I hope so," she murmured. "But I should have trusted you more. I shouldn't have stripped and got on the bed, made you think I was Easter. That was wrong. And then the way I tried you out—I never worked so hard in my life, trying to get you to do it to me when you thought I was Easter." She laughed softly, kissed him once more.

He gave a long sigh. "It was the best," he said. "It was the very best. In all the times we've done it, it was never like that." He gave another hard sigh. "Wow!" he whispered. "It was the very, very best!"

She pushed her face under his chin, kissed him on the throat. "I know," she murmured. "It was for me, too. The best you ever did it to me. It—it was almost more than I—I could stand without yelping. I wanted to yelp. Only I was afraid Papa might hear."

"Papa?" he asked, holding her close.

"He's waiting for me out by the straw stack. I left

128

him there to come see who was in the house. We saw somebody pulling down the window blinds. I thought it was Easter. Papa said it was that streetwalker, Aggie."

"But—but I thought—"

"Oh, that was a long time ago—Easter locking Dora and me in the meat house," she said. "We weren't in there very long. Papa came down for some ham and let us out. But—Walt's got Dora."

She told him all that had happened then, all that he did not know about; and finally she said, "Walt's in the meat house with the others. Papa saw him carry Dora in there, sneaked up behind him and bolted the door. So, you see, everything is okay now. All that's left to do is for us to get word to the sheriff. And Papa will do that—he'll drive to town in one of those nice, shiny sedans parked out by the barn, and do it."

"Easter's not locked up," Jodie said. "We'd better make sure where she is and that she's not going to cause us any more trouble, before we let ourselves relax."

"Easter won't cause any more trouble," Ruie assured him. "She was dangerous only when she thought she might rook Walt out of the ransom money and get you to drive her away from here. And those two things are impossible now. Walt's locked up in the meat house and likely has the ransom money with him. And you— you're locked up in legs and arms and heart, and she'll never, never get you." She laughed softly, and they kissed.

They were still kissing when a flashlight beam struck them from the window that opened on the porch roof, and a voice they knew only too well said, "Oh, Ruie, you're naked! Just look at you! Shame on you, Ruie! And, Jodie, just look at you! You ain't got any pants on! Oh, Jodie, how awful! Shame on you for letting Ruie hug you like that, when you ain't got your pants on!"

129

Ruie jerked up to a sitting position and glared into the flashlight's beam. "Put down Papa's flashlight and get away from there, hussy!" she said. "You do, or I'll come out there and give you some more of the same I gave you awhile ago. Besides, the last time I saw you, you were naked, only you didn't have a man around to appreciate it."

"I'm not naked now," Easter said. "I got a gun, and I got fifty thousand dollars. I'll have a man to help me spend it, too, in a couple of minutes. A real man, a man with guts. Go ahead, you two little calves—go ahead and lollygag. You'll never see little Easter again, and that'll be just too nice—for little Easter."

She turned from the window, snapped off the flashlight and threw it into the room. Jodie and Ruie stood up, and were on their feet in time to see her disappear over the edge of the porch roof.

"She did have a gun," Jodie said. "She must have got in the house somehow. The last time I saw that gun, it was on the kitchen table."

"Let her go," Ruie said. "She's only bluffing. She's got a gun, but she doesn't have fifty thousand dollars. She's just sore. She'll get over it."

She rose, stepped over a bed rail, felt with her foot for the flashlight. "We'd better get some clothes on and go tell Papa everything's okay," she said.

Jodie grunted assent. He went over to the window. Ruie started to say something to him, but cut it short as he leaned far out the window. "Easter doesn't know Walt's locked in the meat house," he said. "We should have told her."

"Why so?" Ruie asked, going to join him.

"Because she thinks only Gary and Buzz are in there," he replied. "And there's a chance she might be telling the truth about having the money. If she is, she'll want a man to drive it and her away from here. Seems to me, Gary'd be her choice."

130

"But she hasn't got the money," Ruie said. "Surely she hasn't—she couldn't have. Walt wouldn't be fool enough to put it where she could get hold of it."

"He might have," Jodie replied, watching the nearest wall of the meat house. "I kind of believe she has it." He wished he could see the meat-house door, but the tree shadow was too heavy there.

Ruie said, "I'm going to Papa's room, find you some decent clothes to wear. You and Papa are near enough of a size; his clothes ought to fit you." She had found the flashlight. Now she turned it on. Jodie saw, as she disappeared into the hall, that she had also found a housecoat, a blue one. The last he saw of her, she was putting it on. "I'll be back in a jiff," she called from the hall.

He continued to watch the meat house, thinking how well everything seemed to be turning out, how lucky he was, and how wonderful it had been awhile ago, with Ruie in his arms. "I guess she'll never doubt me while we live," he told himself. "I guess she'll always trust me, and I know I'll always trust her." He thought, with a slight pang of conscience that he had not always trusted her. He should have known Ruie would not be in the barn monkey-doodling with Gary. But he had not known; he had believed, for a short time, that it was her in there, teasing Gary, refusing to uncross her legs, and Gary playfully threatening to tear her panties off her.

It seemed that that had been a long time ago, and that he had done a mighty lot of growing up since then.

He was thinking that to truly love someone, there must always be complete trust, and that love can never be the beautiful thing it was meant to be until there is complete trust, man for woman, and woman for man, The past night had taught him a great deal. It could be that the past night had made a man of him.

He heard Ruie hurrying down the hall—heard her

say, "I found everything you need, clean underwear, pants, shirt—"

The sound of her feet on the carpet quit with her voice. She went silent. Jodie tensed, crouched forward and thrust his head out the window, listening, as Jason Danson screamed, "Easter! Easter, don't open that door! Easter, Walt's in there! Easter, you get the hell away from that door!"

Jason's screaming stopped, and Jodie yelled to Ruie, "I'm going out the window. I think Easter just let Walt out."

He heard the hard, quick thump of her feet as she ran into the room. He was going through the window, then. "I'm coming with you!" she cried.

He saw a big man in loose dark coveralls as he turned the corner of the meat house. The man was running directly away from him, toward the cow stable. Jodie saw no one else. He headed after the man, short-cutting the path. Tall, dew-wet weeds whipped his bare legs, making him wish he had waited long enough to put on the pants Ruie had found for him.

The man looked back, saw him, pivoted, still running, and lifted his arm. He had a gun. Its report was sharp, flat, like a .32's.

Jodie saw the powder flash, but did not hear or feel the bullet. The man fired once more, missed once more.

Then, up ahead of him, there was another shot, also sharp and flat. The man turned, started on, staggered, fell forward on hands and knees, got up, lurchingly, and went on.

Jodie went after him. "Walt," he told himself. "Easter shot him."

Walt disappeared around the south corner of the cow stable. Tall weeds and thick brush on that side, and the stump of an old, partially tumbled-down silo. The area was strange to Jodie. He knew the other side, the path

132

side; he had traveled that way several times, going to and from the straw stack. He went fast through the weeds, plunged into the brush—almost fell into a deep, stone-walled pit—a manure pit. He caught himself just in time, after teetering on its edge for several seconds. Across the pit, between him and the old silo, he saw Walt, standing at the edge of the manure pit, pointing his gun at a big brush clump.

He heard Walt say, in a high-pitched, rasping voice, "I heard you tell Gary you've got my money. I should've known it was you, you little sneak! It's my money. I risked my neck to get it. You give it to me. Sis, you give it to me, or, by God, I'll—I'll—"

A gun cracked. Powder flame lighted up the brush clump. "The fool," Jodie muttered. He saw Easter, then. She was naked. She came from the brush clump, holding the gun straight out in front of her, pointing it at Walt's head. She moved slinkingly, in a low crouch. And for an instant, the thought that she was too much like a panther to be human went through Jodie's mind.

"You dirty kidnapper," Easter said. "That money's not yours. You stole a girl to get it. It's mine. I found it. I came by it honestly. Finders keepers, losers weepers. Remember how we used to say that when we were little squirts, brother?" She laughed. "Remember, big brother—finders keepers, losers weepers?"

Walt held his gun in his right hand. He tried to lift it, aim it. He tried three times, but each time there was only a small jerking of his arm. The third time he tried and failed, he screamed, "You bitch! You crazy little killer!"

Easter shot him again. He stood there for a moment, seeming to grow taller and taller. Then he toppled over backwards and fell into the manure pit. He screamed as his body made a loud splash in the pit's slimy, watery contents. He screamed again, then he began yelling words. "Sis! Sis, for God's sake, help me! I'll drown in this stuff! Help me! I'll drown!"

Easter ran to the edge of the pit. She was squatting, trying to see into its dark depths, when Gary and Buzz parted the brush behind her. They moved toward her slowly. Gary was reaching for her when she jerked her head around and saw him. She gasped, then screamed.

Jodie was running in the shadow of the old silo then, straight toward her.

Buzz saw him first. "Look out, Gary!" he yipped. "It's the football punk!"

Gary let go of Easter and whirled—and Jodie hit him in the face.

It was not a real good punch—he was moving in too fast. It mashed off Gary's left cheek, taking some skin and meat with it. Jodie tried to throw his left, but Gary got an arm in the way. Jodie pivoted, wanting to see where Buzz was, and Gary caught him in the shoulder with a hard right. The blow drove him back two steps. Buzz was on his left then, and hit him in the face while he was getting his balance. He went down in the brush on his knees.

Gary jumped at him and kicked him in the chest. He grabbed the foot that kicked him, lunged straight up with it in his hands. Gary gave a yell, trying to stay upright on one foot. Jodie jerked, shoved, then ducked as Buzz drove a killing right hand at his head.

He jerked, shoved again, then let go. Gary went over backwards, rolled, almost into the manure pit. Buzz kept him from it, leaping and squatting and snatching. He had a hand on the seat of Gary's pants, was yanking him back off the pit's edge, when Jodie kicked him in the back of the head. Buzz let go of Gary's pants, and would have fallen headfirst into the pit himself, if Gary had not seen him in time, reached and given him a backward shove.

As the shove sent Buzz back from the pit, Jodie

134

kicked him again, in the back of the head. Buzz sagged down on his back, and Gary lunged at Jodie. Jodie caught him coming in with a left on the jaw, then stepped back as Gary fell. He moved several steps into the brush, his knees rocking beneath him.

Easter was standing only a few feet away, standing on the edge of the pit wall, still trying to see what was happening in the darkness below. Jodie went to her, took her by the arm. She did not look at him, but jerked her arm away. "I—I shot my brother," she muttered. "I shot him three times, and he's down there. I—I killed my own brother—"

"You're not sure," Jodie told her. "He might be alive. Ruie will be here in a moment with the flashlight, and—" He turned, stared across the pit. "My God, where is she!" he muttered. "She should be here! She should have been here a long time ago!"

He forgot Easter and Walt—forgot everyone in the world except Ruie. He ran as hard as he knew how, around the pit, back through the brush and weeds the way he had come. He was so intent on getting to Ruie, finding out what had happened to her, that he did not hear Gary coming after him—did not know Gary was anywhere near, until someone jumped on him and grabbed him from behind.

He tried to turn around, tried to strike back across his shoulders, using both arms, and he kept on running. He stumbled, almost fell—then he did fall, intentionally, and rolled.

In a moment, then, he was against the wall of the cow stable, looking up at the dawn-pearled sky, and Gary was under him. Gary was moaning.

He tried to get off Gary, found that he could without any difficulty. He stood up. Gary stayed where he was, with his back against the wall of the cow stable. Jodie guessed he had hit his head on a stone or something while they were rolling, and that he was just

135

now coming to. He got his hands in Gary's hair, yanked him up on his buttocks, then yanked him on up onto his feet.

"I—I didn't hurt her," Gary mumbled, his head lolling, his eyes still glazed. "She ran into the meat house, just as Buzz and I was leaving there. I closed the door on her, bolted it. I didn't hurt her."

"You tried to rape her awhile ago," Jodie said. "You filthy-minded son of a bitch! I ought to kill you. What'n hell did you think you were doing, trying to rape my girl?"

"I—I didn't know she was your girl."

"You knew she was a girl, goddamn you! You've known her all her life. You knew she was good and decent. You low-lifed bastard!" Jodie hit him, mashed his fist into Gary's mouth. He hit him again, driving his knuckles into Gary's eye. He hit him once more, in the belly.

"I ought to kill you!" he said, staring at him, clenching and unclenching his hands, as Gary, wholly senseless now, went down on twitching, wobbling legs.

"If you lied, if you hurt her, I'll come back and kick your brains out!" Jodie said. He turned and ran toward the meat house.

Ruie came out when he opened the door. She had Dora Shetsher by the hand. "Gary locked me in!" she gasped. She felt his arms, his neck, his face. "Are you all right, Jodie? What happened? I almost went crazy in there, wondering—thinking they might be killing you."

"I'm all right, but I don't know about Easter." He glanced past Ruie, into the meat house. "Buzz and Gary are taken care of, for now. How about Aggie and Emma?"

"They're in there. Walt didn't untie them. He wouldn't have untied Gary and Buzz, only he needed them to help him work on the door. They were trying to pry it off its hinges when Easter came and opened it. Aggie

136

told me all about it. You were right, Jodie. Easter wanted Gary to drive her away. She told him so, before she opened the door. She told him she had the money, too. Do you suppose she really does have it?"

"Yes. I think she has it. Come on. She killed Walt, shot him—I think she killed him. He fell in the manure pit. Do you still have the flashlight?"

"Yes. She—she killed him? Oh, Jodie—"

"She shot him three times, after he shot at her and missed. Last I saw of her, she was acting like she was thinking of jumping into the manure pit. The way she was talking, she's sorry now that she shot Walt. Come on, Ruie. She might do anything, anything at all."

"I—I know," Ruie said, holding onto his arm as they ran. "She was always like that—never did care a hoot for anybody except herself. She was always doing things, then being sorry. She—she's just plain no good. She'll always be just plain no good."

Ruie stopped when she glimpsed Gary, lying on his back by the cow stable. Jodie grabbed her arm. "Come on! That's only Gary. He's not dead. I slugged him, is all."

"Oh," she murmured. Then they were running again.

Before they reached the manure pit, they heard a yell from somewhere off ahead of them. "That's Papa!" Ruie cried. "Now what? Oh, Lordy, I hope he didn't try to fight somebody."

The yell came again, full of excitement and fear. Then there were shouted words. "Help! Help! Help, somebody!"

"It is Papa!" Ruie groaned. "Something awful is the matter. Oh, lordy, lordy!"

Jason Danson was on the stone wall that surrounded the manure pit. He was on his hands and knees, leaning far forward and peering down into the pit. He scrambled back, jumped up, when he saw them.

"Easter's down there!" he cried. "She—she jumped in to save Walt! She said Walt was down in there—said she shot him—then she—she just jumped in. Oh, Lord, help us! She was stark naked and had a gun in her hand. She—the poor thing must have gone crazy."

He ran forward, pushed a coil of rope into Jodie's hands. "Do something, Jodie!" he cried. "For God's sake, do something quick!"

Jodie went to his knees beside Ruie, who was already kneeling, playing the flashlight over the dark, bubbly contents of the pit. "Try along the walls," Jodie told her. Ruie nodded, raced the beam across the pit, ran it slowly along the opposite wall.

"There!" Jodie said. "There she is!"

"I see her. Just her head." Ruie gave a long, shuddering sigh.

"Keep the light on her. I'll have to go around to the other side." Jodie was up and running.

"Easter!" Ruie called. "Easter, please answer if you can hear me! Easter, Jodie's got a rope. He's going to get you out."

There was no answer. "Hurry!" Ruie cried. "Jodie, please hurry!"

Jason Danson, crouching behind Ruie, peering over her shoulder, drew a long, whistling breath. "She let Walt out of the meat house," he said. "I saw her, knew she was going to do it. I yelled at her. It didn't do any good. If she hadn't let him out, none of this would have happened. Why did she do it, Ruie? Why did she let Walt out?"

"We think she found the ransom money," Ruie told him. "She wanted Gary to drive her away from here. She didn't know Walt was in the meat house. She thought only Gary and Buzz were in there."

"I yelled at her, told her Walt was in there—"

"I know. We heard you. She didn't believe you, I

138

guess. It's not your fault, Papa. Please, Papa, just keep still. Please!"

"It is my fault," Jason complained, cursing himself for a fool. "I told Walt he could bring the girl here, leave her here till he got the money. It is so my fault."

"Please, Papa!"

"I see her," Jodie called, a moment after he knelt at the pit's edge, just opposite Ruie and Jason. "She's not holding onto anything. I think she's standing on something, a rock maybe—something solid—maybe a part of the wall that fell in."

Jodie was letting down the rope as he spoke. He had made a slip-noose in the end of the rope.

"Easter—Easter, you can hear me. Don't be a fool. You can see the rope. Put the noose over your head, under your arms. Easter I see you. I know you can hear me. Put the noose under your arms. Don't just stand there in that stuff!" He stared at her, dangled the noose in front of her face.

Easter's head did not move. She seemed to be staring at the wall of the pit, which was no more than three or four inches away from her face. The dark, slimy stuff of the pit hid her completely from her neck down. It could have been, the way it appeared to Jodie, that just her head was down there, floating on the black slush.

"Easter!" he cried, becoming exasperated. "Take hold of the rope! Put the noose under your arms!"

Easter's head did not move. She seemed not to have heard a word he said. She only stared at the wall.

Jodie gave Ruie a helpless, troubled glance, then glanced at Jason, wondering what to do.

If Easter would not cooperate with them, someone would have to go down after her. He started to ask Janson if there was a ladder around that could be used for climbing down into the pit; but he stopped, for just then he realized the terrible mistake he had made—that

he, Ruie and Jason had made. All of them had forgotten completely that Gary and Buzz were still free and
dangerous. They had forgotten Dora Shetsher, too; for
none of them had noticed that Dora was not here, had
not ever been here.

10

JODIE stood up quickly and tried to see the spot in the
brush where he had left Buzz lying, unconscious. The
place was some twenty feet beyond Jason and directly
behind him. He told Jason, "Look in the brush behind
you. Tell me what you see."

Jason turned, took a few steps, and stopped, head
outthrust, peering. "Brush is mashed down like horses
been tramping in it. Don't see anything else."

Jodie spoke to Ruie. "We're in trouble. Dumb fool me,
I didn't tie Buzz or Gary either. Buzz was in the brush
over there, unconscious."

Ruie got onto her feet quickly, ran the flashlight over
the brush. Nothing.

"You're not the only dumb fool," Ruie told Jodie.
"We all forgot them. We were too excited over the
shooting, Walt and Easter being in the pit to remem-.
ber. Jodie, do you think they'll cause more trouble?"

"They will," he said. "They know Easter has the
money. They must have got hold of Dora. Has anybody
here seen her since she came from the meat house?"

"She—she came out of there with me," Ruie said,
looking all around. "But I haven't seen her since. Maybe
I did, but—but I don't remember. Not for sure."

Jodie stood still, not knowing what to do, feeling his
youth and inexperience more bitterly than ever. He

closed his eyes for a moment and cursed himself silently, severely.

He still held the rope. It still dangled in the pit. Suddenly there was a slight jerk on it. Then, before he quite realized what had happened, Easter's voice came up to him, saying:

"I put the noose under my arms. Please, Jodie, pull me out! Oh, this awful stinking place! Oh! Oh!"

He pulled her out, not gently, wondering if she had been stalling, if she had known that he had failed to tie Buzz. "She must have seen Buzz there in the brush," he told himself. "She saw the fight. She was right by us all the time. She must have known when Gary took out after me."

Ruie and Jason were beside him when he helped Easter up over the pit wall, took the noose off her. She stood there looking at them, dripping black slime. "It'll wash off, I guess," she said, looking at Jodie. "All I need is a dip in the creek, and the sooner I take it the better."

"You can wash that stuff off in a tub in the house," Jason told her. "You're naked. You ought to be ashamed. You get on to the house now. I'll go with you."

Easter looked at him and smiled. "I'm going to the creek," she said. "Then, when I'm clean, I'll go to the house and pack my things. I'm leaving here, Papa. I'm leaving here right away, this morning."

"You're doing no such thing," Jason told her, firmly. "You're going to—"

He went silent, stiffened, as, behind him, in the brush, Gary Summerfield said, "She's telling the truth, Mr. Danson. She's leaving here, all right—with me."

Jodie stepped past Jason, started around the pit. Gary stopped him, appearing from the brush just then, a gun in his hand. "You stay where you are, football punk," he said. "Take another step, and I'll blast a hole through your empty head." He laughed then, mockingly. "You're the one dumbest no-good kid I ever did see."

Easter flirted her head, smiled at Jodie. "You sure must be a real good football player," she said and walked past him, going on to the path that led toward the house around the cow stable.

Jason started to go after her, but Gary stopped him. "You stay put, Mr. Danson," he warned. "You don't, I'll just have to shoot you."

Easter, calling from the corner of the cow stable, said, "I won't be long, Gary honey."

"Fine," Gary replied. "Aggie and Emma are right around the stable there. They'll go along with you, sweetie. They'll make sure that you won't be."

"And if anybody wants to know where I am," Buzz said, stepping from the brush behind Gary, "I'm right here." He had a gun in his hand. He grinned across the pit at Jodie. "You're the most accommodating fellow I ever met," he said. "So I been thinking—I'm going to do you a big favor. I'm going to kill you last—let you stay around and watch me kill the old man there, and your girl friend, and Dora Shetsher. I'm going to give you some real big juicy kicks. You just wait and see."

It was all over, Jodie thought, glancing at Ruie—all over but the dying. Easter would go wash herself in the creek, dress and pack her things, get the ransom money from hiding; then she and Gary and perhaps Emma would drive away. Then, when Easter was gone, Buzz and Aggie would take care of the dirty work—the killings. They would drive away, meet the others somewhere. Jodie figured that was how it would be, and he wondered what would become of the bodies afterwards. Glancing down into the manure pit, he realized that he knew the answer.

Buzz laughed and said, "Look at it good, football punk, real good. It's going to be your grave. But don't fret. You won't get lonesome, 'cause you'll have your goody-goody little wife-to-be right beside you."

"Easter won't let them kill us," Ruie said, her voice so low that only Jodie could hear. "She's got the money and knows they'll do as she wants till she lets them see the color of it. Don't worry, Jodie. She's goofy and all, but she won't let them kill us."

"I wouldn't be too sure if I was you," Jodie replied, guardedly. "The way I got it figured, she won't be able to stop them. She won't even be here when they do it."

Buzz walked around the pit and picked up the rope Jodie had used to fish Easter out of the manure. Gary followed him, but stopped before he was within reaching distance of Jodie. Buzz gave Gary his gun. He said to Jodie, "Put your hands behind you. Cross your wrists."

Jodie obeyed. "Why don't you shoot us now?" he asked. "Why wait? We're real handy to our grave here."

Buzz chuckled. "I'm not going to shoot anybody," he said. "Don't have to. There was an old dog here last night. It growled at me when I first got out of the car. I didn't shoot it. But it won't ever growl at anybody again."

He tied Jodie's hands with expert thoroughness; then he tied Jason's, then Ruie's. As he finished tying Ruie's hands, he leaned over and kissed her on the side of the neck. She jerked away from him. He laughed and slapped her on the buttocks.

Jodie kicked Buzz in the thigh. He turned and slugged Jodie in the face. He laughed then, watching the blood streaming from Jodie's nostrils. "Now we're all going over behind the straw stack," he told them. "The sun'll be up before long, and it'll be nice and shady over there—on the side of the stack you folks aren't resting by." He laughed again.

Jason swore bitterly. He said, "If Walt was alive he'd fix you, you ugly bastard!"

143

Buzz back-handed him across the mouth, and went on laughing.

"Let them alone, Buzz," Gary said. "They've got plenty of hell ahead of them, no need to give them any extra."

Buzz stopped laughing and looked at Gary curiously, then reached for his gun. Gary gave it to him willingly.

For a moment Jodie thought Gary might be going over to their side, but when he saw him surrender Buzz's gun, he changed his mind. Gary would go along with Buzz. Maybe he was only remembering that he had been a friend of the Dansons once upon a time.

It was full daylight by the time they reached the straw stack. Cows in the stable lot were bawling to be fed and milked. There was a busy stir in the henhouse—hens clucking, cackling, and now and then the rooster crowing.

The farm stock were wanting and needing man's attention. Even old Rub, off across the road in his pasture, voiced a loud bellow every once in a while.

Buzz told them to sit down with their backs to the stack. As he tied their feet, he said, "I'm not going to gag you now, maybe I won't at all—unless you start hollering. I'm going to tie you together, though. So there won't be any heel-and-shoulder crawling away from here, like there was last night." He laughed and looked at Jodie. "Walt saw you make that heel-and-shoulder trip to the meat house. He let you do it, then hit you in the head with a rock. He was telling us about it."

Jodie said nothing. He had not told Ruie how he had got free after Walt had slugged and tied him; he guessed she and her father were wondering what Buzz was talking about. Buzz was passing the rope around Jason's chest, when the old man cautioned him, saying, "My reading specs are in my shirt pocket. Just be careful you don't smash them, huh?"

"Sure thing," Buzz said. He pulled the spectacles from

144

Jason's shirt, looked at them, and dropped them on the ground. "You won't ever need them again, old man," he said.

Aggie came just as Buzz finished tying the prisoners. She sat down near them and leaned back in the straw. Buzz grinned at her. He said to Jason, "She's going to watch you folks till we're ready to leave. And we're going to leave, every one of us, and we're going to leave you right here, alive." He looked at Jodie, then Ruie, grinning broadly. "That's how it's going to be. And you'll all be dead within an hour after we go. Figure that one out." He winked at Jodie. "You figure it out, high-school boy," he said.

"You talk too much," Gary told him.

"And you butt into my business too much," Buzz said.

Gary grinned apologetically. "We'd better go see how Easter's getting along with her dip in the creek," he said.

Buzz grinned. He went from one to another of his prisoners, closely examining the knots he had tied. At last, satisfied with his work, he straightened up. "Okay, Gary boy," he said, "let's do go and see how little Easter's getting along."

They left finally, with Gary telling Aggie to be sure and keep a sharp watch on Jodie. "He graduated from high school," he mocked. "He's real smart."

When they were gone, Jodie thought about what Buzz had said about leaving them here alive, yet them being dead within an hour. After thinking it over for a few minutes, during which time no one spoke, he told himself, "Buzz and Aggie are planning to turn back when they're a few miles down the road. They'll arrange it so they are in the second car, then Easter won't notice. That's how it will be—Buzz and Aggie sneaking back here and killing us. They mean for Easter to believe we'll all be left here, alive. So that's how it will be."

He closed his eyes and wondered if it would really be so—all of them dead and buried in the manure pit in a couple of hours . . . would it, could it, be really so?

"I wonder what they've done with Dora?" Ruie asked abruptly.

Aggie answered her. "Dora's okay," she said. "She's in the meat house. We're taking her with us. Buzz wants to. He thinks she might come in handy if we get in a jam with the law.

Nobody said anything. Jodie wondered if Buzz might not have other ideas for using Dora, just in case they did not get in a jam with the law. He closed his eyes for a moment, pitying Dora. She was in for a bad time. Buzz would kill her eventually, but before that happened he and Gary would probably rape her, no telling how many times.

"The dirty bastards!" he muttered.

Aggie heard him and gave a little snicker.

Easter wanted them to see the money, especially Jodie and Ruie, but she did not want to see them see it or have them see her; so Gary brought it out to the straw stack, five big packs of it—fives, tens, and twenties. Gary moved it back and forth under their noses—it was packed in a pasteboard box. He laughed, fingered it, gloated over it, then left, and Aggie went with him. As she was leaving, she turned her head and thumbed her nose at them.

"S'long, folks," Gary said. "We're pulling out right soon. You'll know when. You'll hear the cars."

Only Jason answered him. He said, "Gary, your ma and paw knows what you are. They told me they did. They know you're a dirty, thieving, woman-molesting, no-good skunk. They told me, Gary!"

Gary was out of sight then, around the straw stack, moving toward the house. He did not answer.

They waited to hear the cars start up and drive out.

146

Minutes passed. They did not say much. Once Ruie remarked that it would be mighty warm on their side of the stack when the sun really began to beam. Nobody answered.

Jodie figured that some fifteen minutes had gone by when they heard the sound that told them they would never hear the cars start—a sound that shook the earth under them, hushed the hens in the henhouse, caused the cows to bellow and go loping around and around the stable lot, their tails stiff and high in the air.

And when the reverberatons of the sound had ceased, far off in the distance, old Jason looked at Jodie, grinned, and said, "Walt! That was Walt's doings. He made a bomb with some of my stump-bustin' dynamite and wired it to the ignition in one of those cars. Maybe he made two bombs, wired one to each car. I don't know he did it for sure, but—well, I do, though. He meant to kill them, I reckon. He sure didn't mean for them to run out of here before he did kill them, or settle with them one way or another."

Ruie spoke next, also looking at Jodie. "Do you think Papa's right?" she asked, her voice small and dry.

Jodie nodded. "Yes."

"But they're—they're all not dead, surely—even if he is right—" Ruie looked sick, like she might faint.

"Depends," Jason said. "Close as them cars were parked to each other, if they were all loaded in, they all got a mighty jolt. If they ain't all dead, what's alive ain't much, I say."

They were all excited; Jodie noticed it first in himself, then in Jason and Ruie. "It's terrible for me to hope you're right, Papa," Ruie said. "But I—I do hope it. I—I hope they're all dead, except Dora."

She paused, shook her head. "Poor Dora."

"The explosion was heard far away," Jodie said. "It had to be. I guess some of the neighbors will be here pretty soon, wanting to know what happened."

147

"Nope," Jason said. "Don't think so. Everybody around here knows I was fixing to blast out some stumps. I guess everybody for miles up and down the road heard the blast, but I don't figure anybody give it so much as a second thought. Nope, I'm sure the blast won't help us none in the way you're thinking it might, Jodie."

"But somebody'll come along out in the road soon— the mail carrier, or somebody," Jodie said.

"Mail carrier goes by here once a week, on Fridays. Yesterday was Friday." Jason seemed to be listening as he said this.

"Well, maybe we can hold out for a week," Jodie said. "Or maybe somebody we don't expect will happen along."

"Could be somebody like that will," Jason replied, and it was evident, now, that he was listening. "But don't count on it. And don't count too strong on us being here next Friday when the mail carrier drives by, either. We ain't got any food, and, worse, we ain't got any water." He shook his head worriedly. "I don't know, if that blast out there killed all of 'em, we might be in no better fix than we was before."

Jodie did not say anything, but he did not agree with Jason. For one thing sure, if the blast had killed all of them, Buzz and Aggie would not be sneaking back here in a little while to kill them. They would be alive, maybe for days—they would have a chance. Someone might come along in time. They might free themselves. He did not have much hope that they could, but they might.

He started to say that there might have been two explosions and they only heard one, because they had been simultaneous; started to say that the jar from the one might have set off the other, in case both cars were wired with bombs, but he did not get it said.

The cry stopped him. He did not hear the cry plainly, but guessed someone out toward the road had called

148

for help. Ruie heard it, too. "Someone yelled," she said. "I heard someone yell!"

"I didn't," Jason said.

"You did, didn't you, Jodie?" Ruie asked.

He nodded. They were quiet then, listening. And after a few minutes the cry came again. This time they all heard it quite clearly. "A woman," Jason said with heavy disgust. "One of them damn whores. You might know if anybody came through that blast alive, it would be one of them damn whores."

"Be still, Papa," Ruie said. "You don't know who it was—it may have been Dora."

Jason wagged his head back and forth and mumbled.

They heard the cry again. This time it seemed closer. "Must be trying to come out here," Jason said. "Must be hurt bad. Must be crawling."

"Be still, please, Papa!" Ruie said. "You don't know anything about what's going on out there. Please be still—"

The cry came again, interrupting her. It came from much nearer the straw stack this time. And this time it came three times. Each time there was just one word spoken. "Help!"

"I think your father's right," Jodie said. "I figure it's Emma or Aggie. They have voices alike."

Ruie nodded.

The cry came again, and this time it said, "Mr. Danson, the cars blew up! Everybody was killed, Mr. Danson, except Dora and I. Dora's bad hurt, and so am I. I'm trying to crawl to where you are, Mr. Danson. If I can make it I'll turn you all loose. Dora was dying when I left her, I think."

"You Aggie or Emma?" Jason asked.

"I'm Aggie."

"She must have just now got her senses back," Ruie said. "She was dazed and out of her head when she was yelling 'Help, help.' But now she's got her senses

149

back, and she said Dora was alive. Thank God for that."

"If she can make it to us and still has enough strength left to untie us, everything'll be fine," Jason said, hopefully. "Everything 'cept Walt and Easter. Aggie said they were all dead 'cept her and Dora." He looked at Ruie and blinked. "I reckon I ain't got nobody in the world 'cept just you now, Ruie," he said.

Aggie called to them again. She was just on the other side of the straw stack, she said. She did not speak at all clearly. They did not understand everything she said. She said she felt like she was dying. A piece of something had been blown through her shoulder and she was losing a lot of blood. She said she did not think she could crawl any farther. She said she was sorry, sorry for everything. Then she was quiet.

They were quiet, too, for a long time. At last Jodie said, "She's dead, I guess. I wonder about Dora. She said Dora was alive, but she didn't tell us how badly she was hurt. I'm going to call her."

He did, loudly, several times, but there was no reply.

They waited a long time for Aggie to speak again. But no word, no sound, came from the other side of the stack. At last Jodie said, "Maybe we can inch ourselves around there if we try—maybe she's still alive and we can help her if we can get to her. Let's try."

Ruie nodded. Jason said, "I'll try anything. How do we go about inching ourselves, Jodie?"

"Wriggle ourselves, twist and squirm, do anything that will move us all in the same direction at once. Come on. I'll count three, then we'll all sort of surge ourselves to the left."

It took them a good two hours, by the sun, the way Jason figured it, to inch themselves around the stack. But they did it. All of them were drenched with perspiration, panting, and almost exhausted when at last they reached Aggie. Long before they got to her, they knew she was dead. Still they went on. But when they

150

had stopped, and were resting, Jodie said, "It would take us a week to make it over to the cow stable. We'd all be dead before we got there."

Jason started to speak, then stopped, noticing that his spectacles were fast to his pants leg. He shook them loose. Jodie and Ruie saw him do it. "Wonder I didn't smash them," he said, "dragging them all the way around here. Some ways, I'm lucky, I reckon."

The spectacles had fallen near Jodie's feet. looking at them, Jodie happened to think of something Buzz had said last night, while Jodie and Easter were hiding inside the straw stack, and Aggie had asked Buzz for his cigarette lighter. What Buzz said then might have saved Jodie's and Easter's lives, and Jodie remembered how relieved he had been to hear Buzz say it.

He went on looking at the glasses, thinking of how it had been inside the stack, with Easter trying to force him to make love to her. It was difficult for him to believe that Easter was dead—that anyone so alive, so vibrant, so passionate, could just not be any longer.

"It's—it's awful," he murmured, looking at Ruie. "Easter, Walt, gone . . . I—" He went silent, jerked his head around and stared at the spectacles.

"What's wrong?" Ruie asked, alarmed.

"I can pick up those spectacles with my teeth," he said. He looked at her, at Jason. "I can. I'll prove it to you."

"But—Jodie," Ruie said. "Jodie, it—it doesn't matter if you can or not. Jodie, are you all right?"

"Yeah," he said. "I'm all right. I'm fine now. I got to pick up those glasses with my teeth. I got to put them back there, behind us." He made a backward motion with his head as he said this.

"But why? Jodie, oh—"

"I'm okay," he assured her. "Don't worry. Listen. I'll tell you what I'm going to do. You two have got to do your part. First I pick up the glasses with my teeth, then we all inch ourselves backwards until our backs touch the stack. It isn't far. We can do it, even if we are tired out. Then I'll turn my head, and—well, just wait. I'll show you."

They were staring at him, sweaty, dirt-streaked faces stiffly curious, eyes wondering, but hopeful. He grinned at them. "We'll all have to bend over at the same time," he told them. "Come on; when I say go, everybody bend. Now. Go."

They bent over, and he did it, did it quickly and without much difficulty. They straightened up. He held the spectacles in his mouth, like a dog with a bone, and grinned at them. He motioned backwards with his head. "Inch!" he mumbled. "Everybody inch!"

It took them only about a minute to wriggle backwards to the straw stack. When they came up against the straw and stopped, Jodie grinned at them, said, "Now, everybody turn his head to the left, slowly, then lean it forward."

They stared at him, puzzled expressions on their faces. "It's not absolutely necessary," he mumbled. "But it might help just a little."

"Our heads aren't tied together," Ruie said. "Jodie, are you doing this just to divert us, get our minds off the pickle we're in?"

"No," he said. "Watch."

He turned his head. What he did then brought an amazed gasp from Ruie, a muttered oath of astonishment from Jason. When he was finished, when he thought everything was as near right as he could make it, he smiled at Ruie and said, "Now we inch away from here —keep on inching. I think we got enough time, but I'm not real certain about it. If it turns out we don't have, we're dead."

He stared at them, drew a long, deep breath, and said as he let it out slowly, "I can stop it from happening, if that's what you both want."

They stared at each other, eyes meeting and holding. It seemed a long time, that moment of decision. Then Ruie smiled, leaned her head and kissed him, turned her head and kissed her father. "Let's inch, fellows!" she said.

Afterwards, many times, Jason said it took a little longer than an hour for it to happen. To Jodie and Ruie, remembering that terrible time, it seemed a near lifetime. When it happened they suffered, suffered terribly. But they were not seriously injured. There were no lasting scare left on any of them. Still, suffer though they knew they would, when it finally happened they cheered—Jodie laughed, Ruie cried, and old Jason blurted out big, juicy oaths.

At first, when they knew it had happened, there was only a trickle of smoke, spiraling upward from the very center of one of the tiny, fiery spots in the straw. Then another trickle of smoke went spiraling up from the other tiny spot. Then, quickly, the trickles grew and completely concealed the lenses which, with the help of the sun, had created them. Then, when the small, twin tongues of flame licked up in the smoke, enveloped and destroyed the spectacles—they then knew, and cheered.

In less than a minute the straw stack was afire and roaring, sending a huge column of milk-white smoke higher and higher into the still summer air.

"It worked, by God!" Jason shouted. "My reading specs brought down the heat of God and set the straw stack on fire! It worked! Hallelujah!"

And later, when they were suffering, holding their faces and hands as far from the awful heat as possible, and Ruie was crying and Jodie was trying to soothe her with kisses, Jason said, "That'll fetch 'em! They'll come now, every man jack, kid and granny of 'em! They'll see it, way yonder over the mountains by Goshawful Creek, they'll see it. They'll think my house and barn and everything is a-burning down. And they'll come,

153

a-hi'sting their britches and their dresses, and a-running for who laid the chunk! Ain't nothing that can happen around here that'll draw folks like a good whopping big property fire!"

And he was right, of course. They came, in cars, in buggies, on horseback, and on foot—off the flats, out of the hollows, down from the hills they came, hurrying. Casey Fenser, his wife and grown son arrived first in their old Jeep. Casey cut the sufferers' bonds. They went into the house and doctored their burns and other hurts. Soon others arrived, and others, and others . . .

Word finally reached the county seat, and the sheriff, with a doctor beside him, drove out to the Danson place. He was followed by an ambulance from the county hospital. The bodies were removed to the county morgue.

The money was taken by the sheriff, kept safely, and returned to Dora's parents when they came to claim Dora's body. But before any of this happened, Jason confessed his part in the kidnapping, first on his knees to God, then to his friends and neighbors, then to Sheriff Bjornson when he arrived. He told it all, not sparing himself or anyone.

"You tried to help the girl at the last," the sheriff told him. "You tried to get her out of your house, to a safe place. I don't think you'll be behind bars very long, not the way you conducted yourself when you realized the kind of people you were dealing with."

The next day a neighbor found Walt's car. He had parked it in a roadside brush clump not far from where Jodie had been forced to park his. And the following day, after the sheriff had said it would be all right, Jodie and Ruie drove back home to Stallerville in it. It was a new car and a good one, but they did not enjoy riding in it much. But they enjoyed something else about the trip very much—once after dark when they parked and

154

left the car and took a long walk in a starbright field, then lay for a long time in the cool, soft grass, and gazed often at the stars—with Ruie seeing them across Jodie's moving shoulder, and Jodie seeing them, looking down into Ruie's eyes.

THE END